THE DOLPHIN'S KISS

DAWN KNOX

British Library Cataloguing in Publication Data A Record of this
Publication is available from the British Library

ISBN: 9798842582969
Formatting and Cover © Paul Burridge at www.publishingbuddy.co.uk
Editing – Wendy Ogilvie Editorial Services

To my mum, Amelia May, after whom I named the ship, the Lady Amelia. And to my dad.

Thank you both for believing in me.

CHAPTER ONE

1790

Jane Moran reached out and with a tentative finger, she stroked the downy head of the sleeping baby.

Hers.

After ten years of longing and crushing disappointment, she was finally a mother.

Abigail May Moran.

Her daughter.

Hers.

Jane was tempted to pick the baby up to hold in her arms but Mrs Riley, the wet nurse, had just settled her and with the infuriating air of someone who'd borne several children already, she'd suggested the little girl be left to sleep. It was probably good advice. Baby Abigail had only been with them a few hours, but on her arrival, she'd filled the house with her lusty cries and Jane had been appalled at her feelings of uselessness and her inability to stop the screams.

"Just hungry, poor little mite." Mrs Riley spoke with the nonchalant air of an experienced mother. "Don't you worry, Mrs Moran, I'll 'ave 'er cleaned up and fed in no time. There's nothing that a bath and a drop o' milk won't mend."

Jane had forced herself to smile whilst resisting the urge to slap the self-satisfied expression off Mrs Riley's face. No other member of her household had been allowed such liberties as the wet nurse – but needs must. The arrival of the child had been so unexpected. Under the circumstances, Jane could allow Mrs Riley a little leeway – even if she was a convict. Regrettably, she'd been the best of the three possible wet nurses whom Jane's husband, Thomas, had managed to find at such short notice. The first had appeared so sickly, Jane had held a handkerchief to her nose throughout the entire interview to ward off contagion. The second had smelt so strongly, Jane had wanted to retch and then, thankfully, there'd been Mrs Riley. The baby took to her immediately, almost as if she knew her.

Jane looked down at her sleeping daughter and, with alarm, noticed her tiny, pink mouth pucker. She wondered if, despite a full stomach, Abigail was about to cry, but the baby's lips moved rhythmically in a sucking motion, and it appeared she was feeding in her dreams.

Such a beautiful mouth.

Such a beautiful face, with long, dark lashes that rested on her cheeks and skin so white and thin, Jane could see the veins in her temples –

blue and delicate.

My perfect daughter.

Not that the baby had been perfect when she'd arrived at the Moran's house earlier that day. She'd been a dirty, mewling scrap of humanity, wrapped in a filthy shawl and clothes that Jane had ordered her maid to burn. And there was that unsightly, red birthmark on the back of her left hand. Mrs Riley, who had an opinion on everything, said it would probably fade in time and not be noticeable when the girl was grown up. She'd remarked it resembled a fish, which had been no consolation. But privately, Jane had been grateful there wasn't more wrong with the child.

When Thomas had told her his friend, Robert Bower, who worked in Government House, had acquired a baby they could adopt, she'd been overjoyed. However, when she'd learned the mother had given birth on board the convict transport ship, the Lady Amelia, during the voyage from England, Jane had doubts. Surely Thomas couldn't be suggesting they adopt the child of a convict – and a common prostitute at that?

But as Thomas had said, "A baby is a baby."

The mother had died in childbirth, so it wouldn't be as if she'd influenced the girl at all. Jane's desperation for a child of her own had won, and now, bathed and fed, the blonde down on the tiny girl's head appeared like spun gold. No one would ever know about Abigail's origins – Jane would see to that. The baby had originally been named Amelia Jackson because she'd been born aboard the Lady Amelia, and her mother, Mary Jackson, had died before expressing a preference for a name. But Jane had chosen names years ago for the children she'd never been able to carry. So, when she and Thomas took their daughter to the church to be baptised, she would be Abigail May Moran and there was no one to say otherwise.

Abigail flexed one hand and Jane nervously touched the tiny palm. The baby closed her fist around her new mother's finger and Jane thought her heart might burst with love and pride.

All Thomas Moran lacked was a son to inherit his hard work. He'd been disappointed the foundling baby hadn't been a boy, but one couldn't have everything in life and the acquisition of the child had thrilled Jane. That was pleasure enough. Perhaps in the future, there would be an opportunity for a baby boy... but in the meantime, there was certainly plenty for Thomas to do so he could secure his empire for a son.

They'd stayed with Jane's sister, Patience, in Parramatta while their house in Sydney was under construction although, luckily, they'd moved back into it days before Abigail's arrival. If Thomas hadn't been in town, his friend, Robert, may not have thought to offer him the baby. It was also fortunate that Jane had spent most of her time in Parramatta, so no one in Sydney would have noticed the sudden and unexpected appearance of a child. All except the servants, of course.

The maids and Cook were the only people who would notice a baby had suddenly appeared, so Thomas gathered them together the evening of Abigail's arrival and stressed there would be an instant dismissal for anyone who gossiped about the new baby, pointing out that he had influence at Government House... He left the threat hanging.

However, a few days later, Jane stumbled into his study in floods of tears. She'd overheard Cook offering her opinion on the baby's birthmark. "No good will come of taking a child from one o' them whores, you mark my words! Bad blood will out! You only have to look at the bairn's hand. It's the sign of the devil! It won't matter that we've said nowt to no one. It'll be obvious where she came from when the world sees that mark!"

Within the hour, Thomas had arranged everything. Cook had packed her bag and gone. Behind her, she left rumours she'd been accused of theft and accordingly, she'd been transported to the penal settlement on Norfolk Island, over a thousand miles from Sydney, in the middle of the Pacific Ocean. She was never heard of again.

"No one will know Abigail isn't ours, my love," Thomas assured his wife at dinner later that day, patting her hand. She snatched it away sharply. It reminded her of the baby's hand with that unsightly mark. It was humiliating enough that she hadn't been able to bear a child and fulfil her duty as a wife but how much worse it would be if people knew she'd been given a baby – and not just any baby, but one born to an unwholesome convict strumpet. Jane hadn't considered anything other than the joy of becoming a mother after so many years of longing for a child but now, the disappointment was so great, it seemed to crush the breath from her chest.

Practical Thomas pointed out that the birthmark would probably fade as Abigail grew. Anyway, as a lady, she'd be required to wear gloves for much of the time, and therefore if there was a residual mark, it would be hidden from society's view. That went some way towards calming Jane's worries.

"There's nothing to fear, my love," Thomas said, "although perhaps I should have waited until dinner had been finished before I dismissed Cook. This fish is too well-done for my taste. But tomorrow, I'll find another cook... And trust me, after my quick action, tongues will not be wagging in this house. Robert Bower can be relied upon not to tell anyone, so the secret is safe."

Jane was reassured until several weeks later on one unfortunate trip into Sydney when, from her carriage, she observed a slattern plying her trade. As a group of sailors passed, the girl flicked her skirt up to show more than was modest and Jane had averted her eyes not wishing to be humiliated by the disgraceful sight.

And then a thought sliced into her consciousness and for a second she felt as though her heart had stopped. Baby Abigail was only a few weeks old, but now Cook had implanted the idea that, 'Bad blood would out', Jane couldn't forget the blood of a prostitute ran through her baby daughter's veins. Would it somehow taint the child? Jane vowed to herself and to the world that she would *not* allow that to happen. Abigail was hers. She and Thomas hadn't come this far for a fallen convict's blood to destroy everything in their future.

Jane would simply not allow anything to go wrong .

Chapter Two

1796

"Abigail! How many times do I have to tell you? Use your right hand!" Jane had silently entered the schoolroom in Westervale Hall, behind the tutor and her six-year-old daughter. She glanced reproachfully at Mr Green, who, in her opinion, was too lenient by far.

"You must prevent Abigail from using her left hand," Jane said through gritted teeth, knowing she'd told him many times before. Everyone knew that using the left hand was merely a habit. Children could adapt to anything, and given a little persuasion, Abigail would eventually become accustomed to using her right hand. She'd be thankful one day because life would be much easier if she conformed. There was also the problem of the dreadful birthmark... When Abigail finally favoured her right hand, the blemish wouldn't be so frequently on display. But of course, she hadn't mentioned that to Mr Green. Not that she had to justify herself to one of her husband's employees. It should have been enough that she'd given him an order.

As Mr Green enthusiastically showed Abigail an illustration in her book, she pointed at the image and then hastily retracted her hand with a guilty glance at her mother. She'd used her left hand. Why did she always act without thinking first? Jane sighed. Mr Green hadn't reprimanded her, indeed, he seemed not to have noticed. His animated expression suggested he wasn't being deliberately disobedient – simply distracted – although it was hard to be certain.

Jane's father had been a cordwainer in London, making shoes and selling them in his shop. He'd earned a good living but even so, his wife had managed their modest house with only one servant. So, when Thomas had first shown Jane the plans to develop their house into the impressive building he intended to call Westervale Hall, she'd wondered how she'd cope with all the work that such a huge house would demand. She'd been hurt when he'd laughingly told her she could have all the servants she liked. He'd reminded her there were many convicts who'd served their time or had a ticket of leave for good behaviour who'd be desperate for such a position, but Jane had been too proud to tell her husband the thought of living in a house with strangers had filled her with horror. And knowing she'd have to manage them and keep their respect, merely added to her alarm. Now, of course, it was second nature to have servants do her bidding – she'd got used to them and similarly, Abigail would become accustomed to using her right hand.

The one member of the household who Jane definitely wouldn't have chosen to engage, was Mr Green. Thomas had explained to Jane that there were no governesses in Sydney who were capable of teaching a young lady of their daughter's standing, and besides, Mr Green had been recommended by Governor King. But really! What need did Abigail have of learning Latin? Jane would have preferred to find a woman to teach her daughter the skills necessary to run a household, but Thomas had insisted Abigail receive an education.

"She'll never attract a rich husband if she can't talk about literature and keep up with the latest topics," he'd said.

Jane had submitted to her husband's superior knowledge and had secretly wondered if perhaps Thomas found *her* dull and uninteresting. He loved her in his own way, she knew, but the more he socialised with the governor and his officials, the more knowledgeable he became. Jane's father hadn't considered an education necessary for any of his daughters, and her mother had been too busy with the latest baby to do anything other than to demand the older children helped with the chores. Jane, therefore, knew much about how to look after a house – skills she no longer needed as she had servants to do everything for her.

Thomas's family had been in trade too, his father had been a master wheelwright and joiner, and he'd wanted his son to go into the business with him, so there'd been no time for him to learn more than basic reading and writing. And as for literature, Thomas had no more idea about it than Jane. She'd never have dared to voice the opinion to her husband, that the lack of education had done neither of them any harm as now, nearly seven years after arriving in Sydney Cove, they were living in one of the grandest houses the town had to offer. It was probably just as well, as she was sure he'd have a clever reply. Perhaps it was because he mixed with Governor King and the other gentlemen who controlled Sydney and he'd learned from them. He often told her of the witty and intelligent things he'd heard the men discuss after the women had retired to the withdrawing room from the many dinners the Morans attended or hosted. However, other than gossip and complaints about staff, Jane learned nothing new from her female acquaintances. She'd told her husband it was hard to learn from women who looked down on her and tended to ignore her. Thomas had simply pointed out that there was a library full of books in Westervale Hall and that she might learn much from those. Sometimes her husband talked such nonsense! It made her rather cross. She could read and write well enough to manage the household accounts and to correspond with her sister, but everyone knew that too much learning was unhealthy for a woman. Many of those books were so thick, if she'd attempted to read one, she was certain it would bring on one of her frequent headaches or even cause permanent harm.

"Look at the elephant, Mama!" Abigail's excited voice brought Jane back from her reverie. The small girl's eyes sparkled as she showed her mother the picture in the book.

"Miss Abigail has become an expert on the fauna of the African continent," Mr Green said proudly, and his pupil looked up at her mother as if seeking a sign of her approval. Jane tried not to purse her lips, but really! Not only was the foolish man ignoring her wishes, but he was also filling Abigail's head with nonsense about animals. And not any useful animals, but ones that roamed a land far, far away.

"Good," Jane finally managed. She noticed her daughter slide her left hand behind her back as if attempting to show her mother she had every intention of using her right hand. For some reason, the gesture brought tears to Jane's eyes.

"I'm trying hard, Mama."

"Yes, yes. Well, try to do better, my love," she said patting Abigail's head awkwardly.

Jane swept out of the schoolroom, closed the door and walked along the corridor. She paused at the top of the grand staircase and looked down towards the marble entrance hall. Behind her, the sounds of Abigail's excited squeal and laughter accompanied by Mr Green's chuckle drifted along the corridor. In the entrance hall below a maid hummed while she swept the floor, and further off, Cook scolded someone in the kitchen. Jane lived in a world of busy activity from which she was – not exactly excluded, as she was the mistress of all of them – but unwelcome. As soon as she appeared anywhere, the atmosphere changed, people sprang to attention – even her own daughter – and then when she left, everyone relaxed. It seemed she'd always been an outsider. Years ago, when she'd been living above her father's shop, her mother had been too preoccupied with her ten brothers and sisters to pay much attention to Jane. Only her younger sister, Patience, whom she'd looked after, had any time for her. Now, although she knew Thomas loved her, he was busy and often away. Indeed, he was currently planning a business voyage to London. And as for Abigail, her longed-for daughter, she didn't seem to need her mother at all. Jane would go further – it seemed she found her mother's company distinctly uncomfortable.

Well, so be it. She'd do her best for Abigail and that would involve finding a suitable husband for her. It would be a great relief because once Abigail was married, it would be her husband's duty to control her.

Heaven help him! The six-year-old girl had begun to display a stubborn, wilful streak.

Abigail had been such a good baby, adored by everyone. Mrs Riley, the wet nurse, had cried when she'd been dismissed although Jane had been happy to see her go. There had been something slightly unsettling about the woman who she later discovered had been Abigail's wet nurse on the Lady Amelia. Mrs Riley had given birth two days before Abigail had been born, but her son had died, so a special bond had developed between the two. No wonder Abigail had settled into her arms so peacefully from the start. Although at her initial interview, Mrs Riley had omitted mentioning she'd been on the Lady Amelia and Jane felt as though she'd been tricked. Occasionally she allowed herself to admit that Mrs Riley had not attempted to conceal the fact that she was a convict and if she had failed to mention the ship she'd arrived on, it may have been because she considered it of no account.

Jane had noticed with dismay, the change from contented baby to a young girl who increasingly showed less inclination to obey and often tested her mother's patience. By chance, Thomas was never there when this happened – or perhaps the girl waited until he was gone – but it was always left to Jane to be the disciplinarian.

Below her in the hall, the maid stopped humming, the swish, swish of the broom against the marble floor ceased and her footsteps could be heard as she headed towards the kitchen. Jane cleared her throat and the girl's head snapped back as she looked up the stairs, eyes wide with fright.

"How many times do I have to tell you, girl? Sweep the corners as well!"

"Yes ma'am, sorry ma'am!" The girl hurried towards the corner she'd missed and with her head down, she brushed vigorously. The swish of the broom was now the only sound that drifted up the stairs. Well, Thomas didn't pay the girl to hum, he paid her to clean, and Jane would do her best to make sure he got value for money. Westervale Hall would be perfect.

Jane would make sure of that.

1807

Having ordered the carriage driver to stop, seventeen-year-old Abigail climbed down and ran towards the young boys who were taunting a cowering puppy. She'd picked the animal up, turned her back on the boys, and was walking back to the carriage before her mother found her voice.

"Abigail! Have you taken leave of your senses? I forbid you to bring that creature into this carriage!" Mama sat forward on the edge of the seat gripping her parasol as if to fend off the tiny, wriggling dog that her daughter held in her arms. "Put it down! It will have all manner of vermin crawling over it! I insist you put it down immediately!"

But Abigail continued to hold the tiny, matted creature that had quieted, and now craned its neck towards the girl's face, its pink tongue darting out, trying to find some skin to lick in appreciation.

It soon discovered its benefactress was wearing gloves, so the licking of hands was not possible.

"Please, Mama! He's starving! I can feel his bones through his skin, I'll clean him up. Please!"

The puppy's tail beat rhythmically against Abigail's skirt.

"Your father will have something to say about this disobedience, my girl," Mama said drawing herself as far away as she could from her daughter, who, still holding the dog, began to climb into the carriage. Seating herself, Abigail smiled down at the dog, allowing it to lick her chin.

She'd made up her mind, this tiny animal she'd spotted cowering from its tormentors by the side of the road would be hers. How could the boys have been so cruel? And now, how could she simply pass by and ignore the dog's plight? She would nurse it back to health and then she'd love it unconditionally, despite it being what her mother would undoubtedly call 'below their dignity'. She wasn't sure how an animal could be beneath anyone's dignity, but she expected Mama would find a way of justifying her opinion. After all, she'd taught her daughter that the only people who were of any significance were those who belonged to the upper echelon of Sydney society like the Morans – the governor, of course – and a few other notable and prominent families. Convicts and the natives who'd been on this land for years before the English settlers had arrived were of no value at all.

Mama pulled her skirts further away from Abigail and the puppy, holding a handkerchief to her nose.

It was a strange little ritual they went through each time Abigail decided she wanted to do something. Her mother would object most strongly and forbid her daughter to continue. If Abigail persisted, Mama would bluster and threaten to tell Papa, but she'd stand back and watch as Abigail carried on regardless.

Finally, her mother would purse her lips and flare her nostrils. Through narrowed eyes, she'd regard her daughter with an air of righteous indignation as if faced with an oncoming storm she was powerless to stop. If she'd ever carried out her threat to tell Papa, he'd never said anything. Abigail suspected that if Mama simply repeatedly forbade her to do whatever she wanted to do, and remained resolute, Abigail would take notice.

Well, possibly... it was hard to say because for as long as Abigail could remember, she'd got her own way. Whilst it was convenient to always win these little tussles, there was something slightly unsettling about it. Several years ago, Abigail had been in her father's carriage when a snake had startled one of the horses, causing it to panic and then bolt. It had been some time before the driver had calmed the horse and slowed the carriage down. That feeling of helplessness, hopelessness, and lack of control had always remained with Abigail. And there was a tiny element of that chaos that accompanied each little argument with Mama.

It was a mystery why her mother invariably opposed her. Eventually, she gave in – but each time, she acquired an extra portion of resentment which were like the bricks her father sold. At first, they'd been arranged side-by-side to make the foundation and then gradually placed one upon the other. The solid wall of resentment was growing faster of late, especially since Abigail had reached the age of sixteen, the previous year.

One evening, shortly after her sixteenth birthday, Abigail had overheard her mother trying to persuade her father it was time to marry her off but, thankfully, Papa had been against the idea.

"Not yet, Jane, love," he'd said, "let's wait a little while. She's hardly more than a child..."

"I don't mean immediately, Thomas, but she needs to marry as soon as is seemly. If you didn't spend so much time away, you'd see she needs someone stronger than me to keep her in line. A husband won't stand for her disobedience. And once she has children of her own, she'll understand..."

"Yes, I know I'm away a lot, my dear, but rest assured, it's you and Abigail I'm working for. I promise I haven't forgotten about finding a good husband for our little girl and I have someone in mind for the future."

"You mean Sir Hugh Hanville?"

"Well, yes, but he isn't *Sir* Hugh, he's the third son of a baronet so his eldest brother will inherit the title. He's unlikely ever to be Sir Hugh. I found several other eligible young men the last time I was in London, but now I'm home I must rely on correspondence. However, in Hugh's most recent letter, he tells me he's planning to come to Sydney. Of course, I invited him to stay with us and he'll meet Abigail then. If he approves of her, we can talk terms and agree on an engagement in the future. But she's still so young, Jane, my love, we shouldn't rush her into marriage..."

It had been the idea that the stranger they'd spoken of would be coming from England to inspect and possibly approve her, that had astonished her.

How could her parents discuss her as if she was a horse to be sold to a new owner?

She calmed herself with the thought that if she didn't approve of *him*, then she'd simply refuse his hand. And that was almost a certainty, as she had no intention of marrying at all.

What would be the point of marriage? This house would belong to her one day and then, she'd do as she pleased, helping all the sick and injured animals she could find. She had no need and no desire for a husband.

As one month turned into another and Hugh Whatever-his-name-was didn't arrive, Abigail forgot all about him.

Now, as the carriage turned into the grand drive of Westervale Hall, the tiny, matted dog curled up in Abigail's lap and laid his head down as if exhausted. She could feel his heart fluttering against her hand as she held the animal steady. Determination to keep him, burned within her.

When they drew up outside Westervale Hall, Abigail gently carried the animal to her bedroom and ordered hot water. She bathed and groomed the dog, feeding him scraps she'd persuaded from a grumbling Cook. "If Mistress ever learns I've given you good food to feed that cur, she'll dismiss me without a second thought."

Abigail's maid, Molly, hadn't taken to the dog but it was she who'd inadvertently been responsible for the name. "He don't leave your side, miss. Funny little black thing. Honestly, he's just like a shadow."

It was true, the tiny animal seemed to have finally found a human who appeared to be trustworthy, and he was not going to leave his new mistress for a second.

Abigail introduced the pup to her father at dinner.

"Shadow? So, now the creature has a name?" Her mother's voice became shrill with outrage, and she looked at Papa for support, but he'd absent-mindedly reached out to stroke the dog's ears.

"Perhaps you should put Shadow on the floor while we eat, Abigail dear," Papa said, glancing at his wife.

Mama's nostrils flared and her eyes narrowed but she said nothing more about the dog.

And once again Abigail realised that she'd won.

However, her triumph was short-lived as her parents' conversation diverted her attention from Shadow despite him repeatedly nuzzling her foot.

"So, he could arrive any day?" Jane's spoon hovered between bowl and lips, and she looked at her husband in panic.

"He's aboard the Pegasus which is due in a week or so. A few weeks at the most."

"That soon?"

"Captain Rainsford arrived in Sydney yesterday and he said he saw the Pegasus still loading cargo in Cape Town as he left. I don't expect it'll be far behind, assuming the tides and weather are kind."

"B...but Thomas! There's so much to do!"

"Nonsense, my dear. The guest bedrooms are now ready to receive people. The house is finished. I know the garden's still not complete but I'm sure he'll excuse that."

"I wasn't talking about the house not being ready, I'm thinking about Abigail. She'll need a new wardrobe at least to meet him..."

Abigail had begun to lose interest, having assumed her parents were discussing a business acquaintance of her father's but as she slipped a piece of bread under the table for Shadow, she wondered why she would need new clothes.

"Jane, my dear! Please calm yourself, there's still time and Abigail has many suitable outfits."

"But not to meet and impress a suitor..."

Suitor! Abigail's attention was now completely on her parents, and she ignored the tiny paw that scraped at her foot requesting more food. Icy fingers of dread spread throughout her body. She'd known the time would come when her parents would find her a husband, but she was only seventeen. It was too soon. "A guest?" she asked innocently, hoping her parents would involve her in the conversation.

"Mr Hugh Hanville is the son of a baronet and we met to discuss a business deal the last time I was in London," Papa paused and delicately sipped the soup from his spoon then dabbing the corners of his mouth with his napkin, he continued "and I mentioned I had a beautiful daughter of marriageable age."

"M...marriage, Papa?"

"Certainly. It's time your future was settled. I have several young men in mind, but Mr Hanville is the first to visit Sydney – and in my opinion, he's the most eligible. If he likes you, it's possible he'll marry you here and take you home to London with him."

"London?" Abigail was appalled at the speed with which things were happening. Usually, she could persuade her father to agree to anything but this time his face had hardened, and she sensed it would be unwise to object.

Mama must have seen Papa's determined look or perhaps she simply took advantage of Abigail's apparent compliance. "You must be ready early tomorrow morning, Abigail, we need to go to town to buy some new garments for you." Mama's tone was firm, and her eyes were challenging.

Abigail forced the meal down without tasting anything. Her thoughts were whirling. If she refused to marry, she didn't believe her father would force her. But she wasn't sure. Nothing like this had ever happened before. Perhaps she was jumping to conclusions. Mr Hugh Hanville might not like her and wouldn't want to marry her.

Or perhaps he would like her. He might be handsome and fall in love with her and treat her like a princess. That wouldn't be so bad. She'd have her own house where Shadow would be welcome, and she'd run her life and her home as she saw fit – with no interference from her mother. So many thoughts and possibilities. So many different outcomes. Common sense told her to keep silent and to curb her headstrong behaviour until she knew more.

Abigail rose early in the morning and asked Cook to look after Shadow. There was no point angering Mama unnecessarily. However, her mother was so distracted during the ride into town, she scarcely seemed to notice her daughter's unusual punctuality and good behaviour.

Abigail knew her father's builders had put the final touches to Hippesley's Emporium the previous week. Situated in the heart of Sydney, the shop was impressive, with large windows displaying fabrics, feathers and trimmings. The proud proprietress, Mrs Elizabeth Hippesley, resplendent in a turquoise gown and matching turban, held the door open for Mrs and Miss Moran and their maids, and greeted them with the utmost servility. A visit from Mama could mean a huge order for goods if a storekeeper was fortunate. According to Papa, Mrs Hippesley had paid a substantial sum to enlarge and improve her shop, so presumably she'd been keen to make up for her outgoings.

"It's very good of you and your daughter to visit my Emporium, Mrs Moran. I hope I can be of assistance to you." The ostrich feather on her turban bobbed and dipped when she nodded politely.

Mama raised her eyebrows as if she doubted the shop could possibly satisfy her needs, nevertheless, she added, "I require gowns and other items for my daughter... But only the finest, mind."

"Of course, Madam," Mrs Hippesley said her eyes opening wide, presumably at the thought of how much such an order might earn her.

"And please only use your finest needlewomen..."

"Most decidedly, Madam, only the best for such a worthy patron as yourself."

Abigail glanced at Molly who was slightly behind her and out of view of her mother's eyes. She saw Molly's lips twitch in amusement and guessed she was thinking about what she'd told Abigail earlier. Elizabeth Hippesley had been a friend of Molly's mother in London, and they'd been arrested and transported together.

"So, your mother was a needlewoman?" Abigail had asked.

Molly had sniggered. "Amongst other things."

It was most annoying. Despite Molly being a servant, she often forgot to treat Abigail with deference when Mama wasn't there. She was several years older than Abigail and having accompanied her mother on a transport ship when she was a young girl, Molly had experienced far more than her young mistress with her privileged and sheltered upbringing.

"I require these items for my daughter," Mama said, handing over a list, "And for myself I will need several new gowns. That lilac silk brocade I believe would suit me well... Oh, and the gold! Yes, the gold is perfect."

Mrs Hippesley called a shop assistant to gather the items for Abigail's approval and took Mrs Moran away to record her measurements and requirements.

Nell, the shop girl, ran her finger down Mrs Moran's list, her mouth working as she laboriously read: gloves, gowns, stays, stockings, petticoats, bonnets, slippers... Her eyes returned to the top of the list and moving her finger to the quantities of each item, she paused at the first.

"Gloves... How many?" Her eyebrows drew together in a frown, and she peered at the paper as if she believed she may have misread the number that Abigail required.

"Two dozen." Abigail stared at Nell calmly, trying to give the impression that purchasing this number of gloves wasn't unusual. Of course, everyone knew that ladies wore gloves when they went out, but Mama insisted that she wore thick gloves all the time, afraid anyone might see the unsightly birthmark on her hand. She made such a fuss, that Abigail was pleased to comply despite finding them so

18

uncomfortable during the hot months. Of course, her mother would consider it imperative that Mr Hugh Hanville didn't see such a blemish on his prospective bride until it was too late. Abigail thought that was unkind. Rather like Jacob from the Bible being tricked into marrying Leah with the sore eyes instead of her sister, Rachel, the girl he'd worked seven years to win.

Hiding her hand seemed deceitful, but if she disobeyed Mama, it would mean trouble. She'd got her own way with Shadow, so perhaps it was best in this instance to do as she was told and anyway, she probably wouldn't like Mr Hanville, so it was pointless feeling sorry for him.

Nell placed several types of gloves on the counter – kid, lace, silk, cotton – and looked up expectantly. There was no point in Abigail choosing the ones she'd prefer – the thin ones that would be cooler – because there was a risk the mark on her skin would show through. Nevertheless, it would be so lovely to have something fine and delicate.

"Would you require them to be embroidered, miss?" Nell asked.

Embroidered? Why not? In that case, she could choose gloves of finer fabric that would be cooler, yet the colourful stitches would obscure anything that might otherwise be visible through delicate material. If she had to wear the dreaded things all the time, why not have ones that were beautiful?

"Yes, please."

"I'll fetch Lottie," the shop girl said, "she does the finest embroidery. She'll show you her work."

A slim girl followed Nell back to the counter, clutching samplers which she placed in front of Abigail. They were exquisitely done. Flowers wove through boughs of leaves, on top of which sat birds and butterflies...

"Do you have something specific in mind, Miss Moran?" Lottie asked, tucking a wisp of fair hair back inside her cap, "Only I have more designs to show you if you don't see anything you like."

"I'm certain I can find something suitable here." It didn't really matter what the patterns were, so long as the stitches concealed the mark on her left hand although, the more Abigail looked, the more she was impressed by the handiwork.

"Did Nell measure your hands, miss?" Lottie asked.

In her haste to be ready early, Abigail had forgotten to bring a spare pair of gloves as a template. She groaned inwardly. Now she'd have to take off her gloves and reveal the birthmark to a stranger – even if she was a shopgirl of no account. But it had to be done. If she ordered two dozen pairs of embroidered gloves that didn't fit, Mama would be

19

furious. None of the pairs of gloves she currently owned was suitable for wearing in the presence of a guest, especially since Shadow had taken a liking to them – or perhaps a disliking – and in the few hours he'd been with her, had managed to chew holes in several of them.

Abigail took a deep breath and began to pull her gloves off ready for Lottie to draw around her hands for the pattern. At least the other shopgirl, Nell, had gone to help take Mama's measurements, so they'd only be on view to one person.

Lottie is a nobody, Abigail told herself. Merely a shop assistant. It is of no account what she thinks of the birthmark. Nevertheless, she knew her cheeks were pink with embarrassment.

As Abigail laid her hands on the paper, palm down, Lottie gasped. Not a tiny intake of breath. No, this was a convulsive effort to breathe.

How dare she make her revulsion so obvious! Abigail's pink cheeks turned scarlet, and tears of humiliation pricked her eyes. What right did this girl have to show such blatant disrespect? Abigail would ensure this impertinent girl was reprimanded for her rudeness. Well, perhaps not. That would mean drawing attention to her mark and that was the last thing she wanted. Perhaps instead, she would... And then all thought of what she intended to do disappeared as she glanced up at Lottie's face... and their eyes met. Abigail had the strangest feeling as if looking at a painted portrait, and then discovering she was staring at her own reflection in a mirror. There wasn't an exact likeness. The locks of Lottie's hair that escaped from her cap were light but not as golden as Abigail's blonde hair and her face had the thin, pinched look of someone who'd known hardship, unlike round-cheeked Abigail who'd never gone hungry. At first sight, there was little similarity between the two girls – Lottie was older, taller, thinner... and yet, against all odds, something about the eyes... the nose... the mouth or perhaps a combination of those features suggested a haunting resemblance.

Abigail was certain that Lottie too, had experienced some sort of recognition as they'd stared into each other's eyes, unable to look away. Abigail's vision blurred and she wondered if she was having some kind of fit, only managing to break the spell by squeezing her eyes tightly shut. She fought the urge to shake her head, much like Shadow when he wanted to throw off excess water. When she opened them again, Lottie was looking down at Abigail's hands but there was no revulsion in her face such as Mama might have displayed. Instead, there was a look that Abigail couldn't identify. Eagerness? But that was ridiculous, Abigail told herself.

"Have you had the dolphin since birth? Lottie asked. Her voice sounded different now. Strained. Almost excited.

Abigail frowned. "Dolphin?"

"On your hand." Lottie pointed to the birthmark and Abigail studied it as if she'd never seen it before. How could the girl have seen the shape of a dolphin inside what Abigail considered a shapeless monstrosity? And yet, when she rotated her hand and viewed it as Lottie had done – as indeed, her mother must have seen it on countless occasions – Abigail could see the arched back, fins and tail of a dolphin as it leapt out of the water. And the more she studied it, the clearer it became. Why hadn't she noticed the similarity before? Why hadn't Mama noticed a similarity?

"Yes, I've had it since birth," Abigail said quickly, her cheeks burning with mortification at the shopgirl's scrutiny and as soon as Lottie had finished drawing around her hands, she quickly slipped her gloves back on.

Abigail lowered her head as if inspecting Lottie's samplers, aware she was looking, but seeing nothing, merely waiting for the heightened colour of her cheeks to fade.

Molly had wandered off supposedly to assist Mama but most likely to gossip with the other maid, leaving Abigail and Lottie alone in the silence that was only relieved by the ticking of the clock on the wall, and the muffled voice of Mrs Hippesley calling out measurements.

"If these aren't pleasing..." Lottie said eventually, her voice uncertain.

"No – yes! What I mean is they're beautiful. But I'm finding it hard to decide." Abigail's mind wasn't on flowers, leaves, birds or butterflies. She'd regained her composure and was now thinking of the birthmark and Lottie's comments about its similarity to a dolphin. If she'd been on her own, she'd have taken her glove off and looked at it again through fresh eyes.

"I could design something special for you..." Lottie said eagerly, "A dolphin perhaps... to celebrate the kiss."

"Kiss?"

"The Kiss of the Dolphin." Lottie blushed. "It's what they say, if you have a birthmark of an animal. It's supposed to have kissed you for luck when you were born."

Abigail frowned and glared at Lottie looking for a sign that she was making sport of her, but the girl's expression was one of enthusiasm and... something else. But what? To Abigail's surprise, she realised it was a look akin to excitement. Well, of course, the girl would be excited, she told herself. An order of two dozen embroidered gloves would probably be quite expensive and Mrs Hippesley would be pleased with any of her girls who secured such an order.

"I would be honoured to embroider a small sampler for you, as a gift, Miss Moran," Lottie said, "perhaps I might include flowers that would be in bloom at the time of your birth?"

But before Abigail could reply, Nell hurried towards them. "Mrs Moran is asking for you, miss. You're to be measured for your gowns."

Lottie looked at her expectantly, presumably wanting to know what to embroider on the gloves.

Not dolphins, Abigail thought. Mama hadn't ever mentioned the likeness, but that didn't mean she hadn't spotted it and there was no point in deliberately provoking her. If she intended to defy her mother, there had to be a good reason because life was going to be fraught enough when their guest arrived; it was best to keep the peace, if possible. And she still couldn't quite believe Lottie wasn't playing some sort of game. All her life, she'd been told to hide the loathsome mark and now, suddenly, someone had referred to it as lucky. And even suggested Abigail had been selected and kissed. It sounded most unlikely. Perhaps, despite appearing to be quite normal, Lottie was, in fact, addled in the head. Skill as a needlewoman didn't mean she could think clearly and besides, she was obviously from a much lower class than the Morans. Probably a convict. One of the lowest forms of life in Sydney. And as for that moment when Abigail had seemed to recognise something in the girl's eyes, that had simply been due to worry and tiredness. Or the heat. Yes, probably the high temperature on the journey into town. It had been unseasonably hot for the last few days. And wearing kid gloves only made her hotter.

"Not dolphins," Abigail said.

Lottie's face fell.

"I will have flowers or butterflies on all the gloves. Waratahs perhaps or any flowers of your choice," Abigail said imperiously, trying to regain some of the dignity she felt she'd lost during such a strange exchange with the shopgirl.

"I will see to it myself, Miss Moran," Lottie said.

CHAPTER THREE

Ahead of Lottie, a wallaby hopped out of the long grass that flanked one side of the dusty track. The animal paused momentarily and with ears twitching and nose raised to sample the air, it glanced warily up and down the road. Fearing she would startle it, Lottie stopped, then watched with fascination as a baby wallaby bounded out of the grass and gambolled around its mother.

Somewhere, far off, a man shouted, and the two animals froze – the small one diving into its mother's pouch headfirst, leaving one spindly leg and its tail dangling. Eventually, the baby managed to drag everything inside and turn itself upright so it could peer out from the safety of the deceptively large pocket. Lottie had seen this happen before, but today she marvelled anew at how such a large, long-legged creature could fit in its mother's pouch. The mother wallaby glanced down at the baby and continued on her way, raising a puff of dust as she hopped into the dense bush on the other side of the road, and was gone.

How Lottie envied the small creature! To have the reassurance that its mother was there to offer a place of refuge at the slightest sign of danger – or even on a whim – would surely be such a comfort and relief.

She'd only paused to watch the wallabies for a minute or so, yet already the early morning sun was burning hotter. Another sweltering day loomed, and once again, the evening would be filled with violent storms. Lottie dabbed at her face with her neckerchief, transferred the strap of her bag from one shoulder to the other and set off again along the road towards Westervale Hall. The bag wasn't heavy since it only contained two dozen embroidered gloves – all completed in record time – and a sampler for Miss Moran, but its bulk lay against her side, making her hot.

As Lottie approached the bend in the path, the trees became sparser, and the harsh sunlight sliced between the branches with dazzling ferocity. She held up her hand to shield her eyes from the glare. They were already sore; red-rimmed and gritty after having worked by candlelight late into the night since Mrs Moran's visit. However, Lottie had been keen to see Miss Moran again and this was the fastest way to do that and to avoid interference from Elizabeth Hippesley or her friend, Susannah Riley. The two women had brought Lottie up and were the closest she had to family.

The convict transport ship, the Lady Amelia, had arrived in Sydney Cove, seventeen years before. Several days before it had docked, Lottie's mother, Mary Jackson, had died leaving her three-year-old daughter to fend for herself. Lottie had been too young to understand why she and her mother had been aboard a ship for so many months, and it wasn't until a few years later that Susannah had explained the Lady Amelia had transferred a cargo of female convicts from England to the newly established penal colony of Sydney. Susannah always avoided any mention of the crime for which she'd been transported but when Lottie had begged to know why her ma had been on the ship, she'd reluctantly agreed to explain.

"Yer ma was found guilty of stealing a cloak and some trinkets what belonged to the wife of one of her regular customers."

Lottie had shadowy memories of living in a large, ramshackle house in Covent Garden and playing with the women who also lodged there while her ma worked. Several of the women had babies, and at a young age, Lottie had learned how to clean and hold them. Of course, she'd been too young to understand then what a bawdy house was and what her mother's work involved. However, having grown up in Sydney amongst women who'd once sold themselves on the streets of London before being transported for various crimes, she soon learned what Susannah meant by 'customers'.

"Yer ma's problems began when her best customer died. That was when his wife found out about his fondness for the ladies of Covent Garden and how often he visited them. When she discovered 'ow much he'd been spending on them, she was furious and wanted revenge. 'E were in the churchyard, so she weren't going to get any satisfaction from 'im and that's when she set out to hurt the girls whose company he'd preferred to hers."

She told Lottie that when the constable had searched Mary's room in the bawdy house, he'd discovered a cloak as well as several rings and brooches that the widow claimed were hers. Mary protested her innocence, telling the constable the man had given them to her, but the courts found in favour of the widow, resulting in Mary and her daughter being sent halfway across the world to serve her sentence.

After Mary's death, Susannah and Elizabeth had looked after Lottie – no easy task as Sydney had endured hard times with food shortages, especially during the early years of the colony. But somehow, they'd undertaken to feed, clothe and house the little girl. When they'd had money, they'd paid for lessons to teach her to read and write. And now, Elizabeth employed her.

For Lottie, it hadn't been the same as having a mother but then, there hadn't been time to dwell on such things. After the two women had received their pardons, Susannah had taken in laundry and as she managed to put money by, she'd rented a few rooms which she'd let out to lodgers. Elizabeth had a market stall from which she sold the clothes that she and Lottie had made. The two women had both worked single-mindedly until they'd saved enough for Susannah to buy a boarding house and her friend, Elizabeth, to purchase the Emporium which had just been enlarged and improved until it was one of the grandest stores in town.

Lottie carried on along the path, leaving the relative shade of the trees, and as she rounded the bend, she halted in surprise. Ahead of her, was Westervale Hall. Set on a rise that afforded it wonderful views of Sydney Cove, the house was breath-taking, and she could scarcely believe that Miss Moran had grown up in such luxury whilst the early part of her life had been spent living in a bark shack. But it wasn't the beauty of the mansion that was making excitement rise in Lottie's chest, it was the thought of finding out more about the girl who lived there.

The birthmark on Miss Moran's hand was exactly like the one Lottie remembered on the left hand of her baby sister, Amelia. Ma had died giving birth to the girl aboard the transport ship, seventeen years ago. When Lottie had been old enough to know about such things, she'd calculated that since the voyage had taken more than nine months, Amelia's father must have been one of the sailors. But who, she had no idea. It wasn't surprising since Lottie had been so young, and yet, she remembered as if it had been yesterday, the tiny whimpering infant being placed in her arms. Around her, the women on board, who'd assumed the role of midwives, tried – and failed – to save her mother's life. As young as Lottie had been, she'd seen enough to know her sister would need her. "I'll take care of you, Amelia," she'd whispered in the baby's ear, "I promise."

Susannah had given birth to a stillborn boy two days before and had offered to feed the motherless baby but shortly before the ship weighed anchor in Sydney Cove, Amelia had died. Lottie had been distraught and Susannah's assurances that she'd gone to be with her mother had done nothing to console her.

"But if Ma took Amelia, why didn't she take me?" Lottie had wailed, burying her face in Susannah's huge bosom. Presumably, she'd worn herself out crying after that as she had no recollection of being taken ashore nor of the following few days.

Living in the penal colony had presented many challenges and during the last seventeen years, Lottie had pushed the memories of her mother and sister into the furthest reaches of her mind. It was a comfort knowing they were there and that she could return to them at will but the hardship of surviving in such a harsh environment had taken up most of her thoughts and time.

However, the sight of the birthmark on Miss Moran's hand had released sharp, intense memories that had spilt out – not softened and rounded like they might have been if she'd often brought them to mind and mulled them over. No, having been hidden away, the raw memories were almost too painful to re-examine.

Once again, she tried to make sense of everything. There could be many people across the world who'd been kissed by a dolphin at birth. And if so, their birthmarks might be identical. Two different girls – one dead, one alive, and both with the same mark on the same hand. Well, why not? The world was full of coincidences.

However, as she'd gazed into Miss Moran's eyes, there'd been the ghost of a memory there; something so familiar she could almost have reached out and touched it. And it seemed as though Miss Moran had recognised something in her too. Or was she simply being fanciful?

Usually, if she had a problem, she'd have talked it over with Susannah or Elizabeth but this time, she'd decided to keep her thoughts to herself. Susannah had explained why Mary Jackson had been accused and convicted of theft but after that, whenever Lottie had asked about her mother, the smile on Susannah's round, wrinkled face would always drop and she'd say, "Let's look towards the future and leave the past where it belongs."

Elizabeth, the quieter of the two, had always nodded in agreement and Lottie assumed that neither woman wanted to remember their old life in England nor their transportation. They were now both independent, and one day, if their businesses continued to thrive, they might even be considered women of means. It was understandable if they only wanted to look towards the future.

That didn't help Lottie, of course, but she accepted it as being a part of her life she couldn't change. Was it possible two people could have the same birthmark? And why had she felt as though she'd recognised something in a girl she'd never met before? If only she had someone to ask. If by some miracle Amelia hadn't died and had been taken from the ship to be brought up by a rich family, why had no one ever told her? One thing was certain, she wouldn't be able to rest until she knew.

The maid led Lottie from the servant's entrance into a large, airy room. Yellow and white-striped wallpaper matched the curtains that hung at the enormous windows through which Lottie could see the gardens.

Here and there in the room, touches of gold glinted – the ornate clock ticking on the table, the gilt-framed paintings on the walls and the golden candlesticks, all mellow in the light that flooded through the huge windows. How different from the gloomy, cramped room where she spent hours sewing by candlelight on all but the brightest of days.

At first, Lottie thought that, other than the maid, she was alone but the sound of giggling and snuffling told her otherwise. She spotted Miss Moran lying on the Turkey rug, tickling the stomach of a fluffy, black dog who nipped playfully at her gloved fingers.

"Miss Jackson from Hippesley's Emporium is here for you, Miss Abigail," the maid announced.

Miss Moran stood up and smiled, and once again, Lottie had the strange sensation she was peering at herself. For a second longer than was usual, their gazes locked and then both looked away.

"I have your gloves, all embroidered as you requested, Miss Moran," Lottie said quickly.

The girl indicated Lottie should place the gloves on the side table. "Thank you. Please leave them there. I shall inform my mother they've been delivered, and she'll be sure to settle the account speedily."

The dog jumped up at Miss Moran and she bent over to stroke its head. It appeared she had no interest in the gloves, nor in checking them, so Lottie laid them out carefully in pairs to show off the embroidery. "I have something else besides... something for you... as promised." She took the sampler out of her bag and held it up for inspection, then seizing on Miss Moran's hesitation, she added, "I hope this pleases you. I tried hard to make it meaningful to you."

The girl took the sampler from Lottie's hand.

"But that is so much like my..." Miss Moran said, looking from her gloved hand to the embroidered dolphin. She half-turned to obscure Lottie's view of her hand as she pulled off the glove and gasped, "It's not just *like* my mark, it's almost identical. How did you do that?"

"I have a good memory," Lottie said, searching the girl's face for signs of pleasure – or displeasure. Miss Moran was frowning, although Lottie couldn't tell if it was because she was puzzled or because she didn't like the gift.

"And you included Waratah flowers," Miss Moran said pointing to the large, red blooms, "they're my favourites."

"Then, I imagine you were born in the springtime," Lottie said, holding her breath. She'd tried to find out Miss Moran's date of birth before by initiating a conversation about flowers but they'd been disturbed by Nell before she could find anything out.

"Indeed, I was! How could you know that?"

"I've noticed people tend to prefer the flowers that are in bloom at the time of their birth," she lied. It wasn't a dreadful lie. And after all, it could indeed be the truth. "I expect you were born in... perhaps... October?" She swallowed and held her breath again. *Please let it be November...*

"No, early in the month of November. The fourth day, in fact."

A harsh grating sound filled Lottie's ears like someone sawing wood. She realised it was her breath coming in jarring gasps and she forced herself to breathe in and then, slowly, to breathe out. *In, now slowly, evenly breathe out* she told herself but still, she was gulping for air.

"Is something amiss? You've become quite pale. Indeed, you don't appear well at all!" Miss Moran said, her face full of concern, "Please sit down until you recover." She turned to the maid who was hovering uncertainly by the door. "Molly, please bring some cordial and smelling salts."

When Lottie was sure she'd regained control of her voice, she said, "I'm fine, thank you."

Now Lottie knew the truth. There was the proof. Lottie's sister, Amelia, had been born on the fourth day of the month of November in the year of our Lord 1790. Each year on the anniversary, Lottie walked down to the harbour on her own and threw two flowers into the sea – one for her mother and one for the sister who'd been born and only lived for a few days. It was a date written on her heart.

Miss Moran had been born on the same day and had an identical birthmark to her sister. A wave of something overwhelming swept through her body. Disbelief? Shock? Rage?

Lottie sank gratefully into the chair that Miss Moran held for her and placed a trembling hand on her chest, trying to steady her breathing. She lowered her head, unable to look into the face of the girl she now knew was her sister, afraid that something in her expression would give the truth away. Like a whirlpool, her thoughts swirled and sucked her deeper and deeper. Lies and deceit? But whose?

Were Susannah and Elizabeth also aware the baby hadn't died? Had they known and kept her sister from her for seventeen years? And who'd been responsible for giving the baby to Mr and Mrs Moran? Did the girl know she was adopted? If not, should Lottie tell her? The whirlpool threatened to drown her.

After Molly had brought glasses of cordial, Miss Moran inspected the sampler once again as if giving Lottie time to recover.

"This truly is exquisite work, Lottie. The ship is skilfully done and almost seems to be sailing on the waves next to the dolphin. You're obviously very gifted." She paused for a few seconds. "Pray forgive me for asking but you don't seem like a convict to me... although," she added quickly, "I know very few and am therefore not a good judge."

Think! Lottie told herself, trying to tame the chaos in her mind. She chided herself for not having thought this through in advance. But she'd hardly dared to believe she'd find her sister alive... Now, how much could she tell this girl? Or *should* she tell her?

Lottie decided on as much truth as possible without revealing the entire story. She swallowed and when she thought her voice was under control, she said, "No, Miss Moran, I'm not a convict. I came with my ma but she died when I was very young."

"And your father?"

Lottie shook her head. "I neither know who nor where he is."

"So, you're all alone in the world?" Miss Moran's tone was sympathetic.

"I was fortunate that two of the women who knew Ma looked after me as I grew up." She paused, wondering if indeed, she had been fortunate. It was possible the two women she'd trusted most had deceived her for years.

Miss Moran took one of the gloves from the table and after inspecting it, she said brightly, "If anybody remarks on the embroidery on my gloves, I'll be sure to tell them who did it and perhaps to send some customers your way. And I'll make sure Mrs Hippesley knows that Mama and I are very pleased with your work. I'm afraid I have no more influence than that, but I will do all I can."

Lottie smiled and a rush of emotion surged through her. At least her sister had a kind heart, wanting to help someone whom she considered a stranger – and less fortunate than herself. Lottie's desire to tell the girl of their relationship was almost overwhelming but she bit back the words. Once they were uttered, there would be no going back and what good would it serve her sister to know her origins? Many lives would change – and none for the better. Now Miss Abigail Moran was self-assured, educated and wealthy – and she had an influential father. What would she have if everyone knew her as Miss Amelia Jackson? Nothing more than Lottie had, and that was little enough. Seventeen years ago, Lottie had vowed to her baby sister she would look after her and now, the only way she could do that was to keep the secret – and keep her distance, however much she longed to know this girl.

"Tell me the significance of these," Miss Moran said, looking once again at the sampler and pointing at the letters Lottie had hidden deep in the leafy trellis interwoven with flowers – MJ, CJ and AJ.

"You have a keen eye, miss," Lottie said, taken aback at how observant the girl was. The initials were not immediately obvious, and she wondered if she'd been foolish to include them. Could she make up something believable? However, nothing came to mind, so she decided on the truth. "If the work is large enough, I often include the initials of my mother, Mary Jackson; my own, Charlotte Jackson and my younger sister, Amelia, who... is no longer with us."

Lottie couldn't meet the girl's eyes. Surely everything must be obvious from her face? To hide her confusion, she bent over to stroke the dog which sniffed her hand and then moved away from Miss Moran to sit at Lottie's feet.

"How remarkable!" Miss Moran said, "Shadow refuses to let anyone touch her except me... and now you."

They discussed the flowers Lottie had incorporated in her sampler and the butterflies on the gloves, then Abigail explained how she'd found Shadow, and the conversation flowed easily from one topic to the next. However, when the clock chimed noon, Lottie realised with a start she was late. Elizabeth had expected her to return much earlier, and Lottie knew she wouldn't be happy.

"Are you certain you're recovered?" Miss Moran asked as she escorted Lottie to the main door, "The day is so hot."

Lottie assured her she was well. Indeed, it scarcely mattered if she wasn't, she'd still have to hurry back in the heat.

"Wait! You must borrow my parasol. It will shade you on your walk. No! I insist!" Miss Moran said when Lottie objected, "Mama and I will come to Hippesley's Emporium within the next few days, so you can return it then."

Reluctantly, Lottie accepted it. She wondered whether it would be possible to leave it outside the front door but that would appear extremely ungrateful. Besides, it was proof of her younger sister's thoughtfulness, and she was grateful for the slight relief it offered from the blazing sun as she set off home to what was likely to be an angry reception. As she walked away from Westervale Hall, tears slid down her cheeks unchecked. For years, she'd held them back, having learned from an early age that crying solved nothing. She'd always tried to make the best of her life. But for the first time in years, she allowed herself the luxury of crying for the loss of her mother and baby sister, and now, for the loss of the girl who would never know they were related by blood.

Chapter Four

Christopher Randall reined in his horse and turned into the imposing drive of Westervale Hall. The harsh noonday sunlight flashed off the many windows of the mansion with diamond brilliance.

One day, he told himself, he would own a house like this. Or possibly something grander. Well, why not? Allow yourself to dream the impossible, he told himself. He was young, energetic and determined. And importantly, he had no ties. No wife or children to consider. If those qualities were sufficient to succeed, he'd already be a rich man but unfortunately, they weren't enough to lift a man out of poverty. The world belonged to the nobility and gentry and if they were willing to offer their patronage, then fortunes could be made. If not, then it would be like trying to sail away in a boat that was firmly at anchor.

During a chance conversation in a tavern, Christopher had learned that a man who'd recently acquired land along the banks of the Hawkesbury River had placed a large order with Moran Building Supplies. He'd also discovered that Mr Moran was looking for a reliable packet service to deliver goods to such remote places.

As more people settled along the banks of the river, they increasingly required building materials for their homes and as their farms began to flourish, the colonists would want to send their produce to market in town before it spoiled. If all went well, Christopher stood to gain two cargoes per trip. Of course, Mr Moran had his pick of men with boats and could engage anyone to convey his goods, but Christopher was hoping his offer to guarantee a service to the Hawkesbury would mean he earned exclusive rights. Other captains were not as brave – or as foolhardy – and so far, no one offered such a service.

Not surprising because it was a perilous journey. Once the boat passed the northern heads of Port Jackson and sailed out into the ocean, it would follow the coast through challenging waters to find Broken Bay and the entrance to the Hawkesbury River. Even when a boat reached the calm river waters inland, there were potential hazards. Occasionally attacks had been carried out by the natives who were gradually being displaced from the land over which they'd once roamed freely. And of course, it was so remote that should an accident occur, it was unlikely anyone would be close enough to offer assistance.

Christopher arrived at the stables and dismounted. "Mr Christopher Randall, come to visit Mr Moran," he said to the stableboy as he handed him the reins.

"Yes, sir." The stableboy touched his forelock and Christopher noted his deference although he warned himself not to set much store by that. He was merely a boy, and Christopher's clothes would have been enough to persuade him he was a man of quality. No, what mattered to Christopher, was whether he could impress Mr Moran.

Already, Christopher had invested a large sum of money in his new vessel and in this proposal. A flowery-worded and beautifully written letter requesting an interview with Mr Thomas Moran had cost more than he'd expected. Christopher had hired a scribe who offered his services to those who needed a carefully worded and well-scripted letter. The man had once been a lawyer's clerk in London who'd been convicted of fraud and had been transported. It hadn't taken him long to work out the significance of this letter to Christopher and accordingly, the fee had risen substantially.

Christopher had grudgingly paid, whilst wondering if he should have taken a chance and written it himself. However, when he read the fancy, formal phrases written in elegant loops and swirls, he knew he'd made the correct decision and thankfully it had done its job because Mr Moran had invited him to his home to discuss business.

But the letter hadn't been the end of the expense. In order to give the right impression, he'd also had to buy new clothes, hat and boots and hire a fine horse but, he knew, he looked every inch a gentleman.

Now all he had to do was to convince Mr Moran he'd be the best man for the job. He must give no clue he was desperate, having borrowed heavily to get this far, and with debts that would soon need to be paid. If he couldn't cover all his expenses soon, his meticulously laid plans would come to naught and he'd end up penniless, once again.

Christopher wondered if his careful and expensive preparation had been necessary. He'd heard that Thomas Moran, despite his wealth, had not been born a gentleman. He was the son of a tradesman and had arrived in Sydney, with great hopes but not much money – just like Christopher. Having borrowed to buy into a brick kiln and other enterprises, Mr Moran had quickly earned a fortune, and if that was true, it might mean that he'd be sympathetic to Christopher's ambitions – with or without new clothes – but then again it might not. Men who'd become successful sometimes resented anyone trying to follow in their footsteps. No, the safest way was for Christopher to give the impression that he was already prosperous and although he wouldn't lie, he would imply that he had men working for him to sail his boat. Ultimately, why would Thomas Moran care who was responsible for the hard work and or who took the risks, so long as his requirements were met?

Christopher straightened his hat looked down at his coat to check for dust and then drawing his broad shoulders back, he knocked at the imposing door of Westervale Hall.

Abigail sat on the window seat of her bedroom, absentmindedly fondling Shadow's floppy ears and staring out at the view. Lottie had left so abruptly and now the afternoon stretched endlessly ahead of her. She wondered whether Mrs Hippesley had been as angry as Lottie had feared she would be at her tardiness. Mama always made such a fearful scene when any of the servants were late, and Abigail found herself hoping Lottie had been able to slip into the shop unnoticed. But one thing was certain, this was not the sort of weather in which to rush anywhere. Abigail had watched Lottie hurry down the drive back to work, the ivory-coloured parasol bob, bob, bobbing, and she could only imagine how hot and uncomfortable she'd be when she arrived at the shop.

As Lottie had neared the end of the drive, Abigail's attention had been attracted by a man on horseback. He'd reined in his horse and had stopped outside the gates, sitting stationary for several minutes, staring at the house. She'd wondered if he was lost or simply passing by and had paused to admire the house. By the time she'd turned her attention back to Lottie, the girl had turned the corner, however, the stranger had urged his horse forward onto the drive.

She hadn't recognised him, even when he'd drawn closer, but he'd sat the horse well and, judging by his clothes and mount, he was prosperous. Probably one of the governor's men or perhaps a ship's captain. Papa often received visitors who came to discuss government matters or business, and she never met any of them, so she probably wouldn't recognise this man. He'd dismounted and led his horse towards the stables, and she'd forgotten about him as the tedium of another afternoon spent alone bore down upon her.

Abigail looked once again at the clock. Only thirty minutes had passed since Lottie had gone. She sighed and picked up the sampler that was lying next to her on the window seat and ran her finger over the neat stitches. She'd forgotten Lottie had said she'd sew something for her. In fact, she'd forgotten all about the gloves and their delivery. They hadn't been something she was looking forward to receiving nor, indeed, to wearing. But now, Abigail regretted her lack of interest when Lottie had arrived. She hadn't intended to be rude, but anything that reminded her of the birthmark caused her embarrassment that she dealt with by feigning indifference. Hopefully, she'd make it up to Lottie by finding her new clients.

Abigail wondered if she ought to fetch her own sewing and continue with it, but the last piece she'd done would have to be unpicked and she couldn't summon the enthusiasm, even with Lottie's marvellous example to inspire her. Mama often shook her head in horror at the mess Abigail made of her needlework – sewing with her right hand was so difficult. But it was a shame that Lottie's talent would be used to merely embroider handkerchiefs, tablecloths... and gloves. She deserved more from life. The time Abigail had spent with Lottie had passed so quickly and so pleasurably. That was puzzling. The girl was of similar status and age to Molly, yet Abigail had little desire to spend time with her maid. However, she and Lottie had spoken easily after an initial disquiet between them which had undoubtedly been due to Abigail's indifference to the delivery of her gloves.

Furthermore, Lottie had demonstrated an appreciation of Shadow and unusually the dog had responded favourably. The only other person who displayed any affection for the dog was Cook but Shadow was wary of the huge woman with the deep, bellowing voice, even if she did save scraps for him. However, Shadow had gone willingly to Lottie and somehow it had reinforced an ease between the two young women that had stopped abruptly when the clock had chimed noon. Lottie had become most agitated when she'd seen the hour.

Abigail bent closer to Shadow. "It's not something we'll tell Mama, Shadow," she whispered into the dog's velvety ear, "she'd be vexed if she discovered I'd spent time in the company of a shopgirl."

Shadow looked up with his soulful, brown eyes and licked her chin.

"Yes, I know you're good company, but sometimes I think it would be nice to have someone of my own age to talk to."

Yes, that was it, she was lonely.

Well, she must be careful. The lack of a companion should not push her into an unsuitable friendship that wouldn't be tolerated by her parents. Abigail felt sorry for Lottie. She'd lost her mother, never known her father and having been transported to a foreign land, the closest she had to family were two of her mother's friends. As she'd promised, Abigail would be generous and try to put business her way. But she was under no illusions that Lottie cared a jot for her. As Mama had warned her, like anyone else of her class, Lottie would undoubtedly have her eye on any opportunity, and Abigail with her rich parents would represent that. As pleasant as the time had been chatting and laughing with Lottie, it would not happen again. Strangely, her stomach twisted with sadness and a sense of loss.

Six minutes had passed since Abigail had last looked at the clock.

A book. Yes, she'd go to Papa's study and ask to borrow a book to read. That might be a pleasant way to pass time. However, when she started down the stairs, she heard voices coming from the study and realised Papa had a visitor. She remembered the man who'd arrived as Lottie was leaving and wondered who he was and the likelihood of him leaving soon.

Next to her at the top of the sweeping stairs, Shadow froze, his ears pricked up, listening. His alertness suddenly jolted Abigail, and with a shiver of fear, she wondered whether this man could be Mr Hugh Granville, or Grenville or some-such-name?

She would have expected her would-be suitor to arrive in a carriage with his luggage, but it was possible that he'd been eager to come to Westervale Hall, and his belongings would follow. Now, she wished she'd taken more notice of the details of his arrival.

The sound of voices grew louder, as if the two men were approaching the door and were about to come out of Papa's study. Abigail grabbed Shadow and fled to her room. She knelt on the window seat to see whether the man was leaving and if he was, if she could spot anything about him that would give her any clues as to his identity.

Instead of going towards the stables, she saw her father and his visitor heading along the path towards the newly finished temple and the half-built fountain. Such structures seemed curious things to have in a garden, as Mama had observed when Papa had suggested them, but he'd overridden her objections, telling her that they were exactly the sort of features that wealthy people built on their estates. Mama's cheeks had reddened but she'd said no more. Abigail knew her mother felt ashamed of her social shortcomings and that she yearned to be as familiar as Papa with what was considered to be à la mode. Shortly after, some of Papa's men had appeared and begun work on the temple and fountain and Mama had not mentioned them again.

Abigail wondered if the young man who was accompanying Papa was one of the masons although that didn't seem likely because he was too well-dressed. A new business partner, perhaps? But Papa didn't usually take his visitors into the garden – not that there had been much in the garden to show anyone before – the paths and flower beds all being new. The most likely explanation was that this man was indeed Mr Hugh whatever-his-name-was. Abigail knelt on the window seat, pressing her nose against the glass pane, and peered through. He was tall and slim, with long legs and broad shoulders that suggested great strength. His long, dark hair was tied back but it wasn't until he turned around, his gaze following her father's finger as he pointed out something in the garden, that she could see his face. It was pleasant... extremely pleasant. Her father had obviously said something amusing and the man's laugh drifted up to her; deep and throaty. What would it be like to stand next to this man and know that for the rest of her life she would be tied to him? Unless of course, he didn't want to marry her... or he wasn't the man at all.

There was only one way to find out – she would pretend to encounter them by accident in the garden. It was her duty to ensure she accompanied Shadow while he was in the grounds and who would know they'd returned from the garden not forty-five minutes past? The dog might want to go out urgently. She checked herself in the mirror and pulling on a bonnet, she tucked tendrils of hair behind her ears, then brushing Shadow's hairs off her skirt, she exchanged her gloves for one of the pairs that Lottie had delivered earlier. She wasn't exactly dressed for company but if she waited to summon Molly and change into something smarter, Papa and the man would be gone. Stooping to pick up Shadow, she hurried down the stairs.

The meeting with Mr Moran had gone extremely well. He'd seemed impressed with Christopher's guarantee that the boat would sail to the Hawkesbury River in any weather.

Whether Mr Moran saw himself in the younger man, recognising his ambition or whether he simply needed a service on which he could rely and thought he could trust Christopher, it was hard to tell. But one thing was certain, Mr Moran seemed to have taken to him. After they'd agreed on a price and shaken hands on their business agreement, he'd insisted on showing Christopher around the garden.

"Come and see my new temple," Mr Moran said proudly, "The men are still working on the fountain, but it's almost finished, and you'll see how the two features complement each other."

Christopher was so relieved that something had finally gone right for him, he was finding it hard to concentrate on garden plans, but he nodded politely hoping his preoccupation wasn't obvious. It was frustrating to know that if he'd arrived in Sydney a few years earlier, he might also have taken advantage of the opportunities that had been seized by men like Mr Moran. Now, Christopher would always be several steps behind. He tried to imagine what Mr Moran might have looked like when he'd arrived. Hungry and dirty like Christopher? Nothing like this stout, well-dressed man who owned a temple, that was certain. Thomas Moran had been in the right place at the right time and Christopher wondered if he had sons ready to step into his shoes whenever it all became too much for him. How lucky they were!

Christopher thought back to his father, but his memories were few. Da had walked out of his life one day and never returned. That had been a good thing for his mother whose bruises had been allowed to heal once her husband had gone, although she'd never regained her spirit. She'd died several months later, and it had been his eldest brother, Robert, who'd held the family together. He'd been a Waterman on the River Thames and had taught Christopher everything he knew about sailing.

Christopher planned to follow Robert's example and somehow scrape together enough money to buy his own boat. Their parents' relationship had convinced both Robert and Christopher that marriage brought nothing but misery and more mouths into the world – and both had sworn never to marry. Rowing on the Thames was physically demanding, and a man had to earn enough to set himself up before his body and strength gave out – not an easy thing to do with a growing family.

However, one cold winter, Robert had caught a fever and several days later, he'd died, leaving everything, including his boat, to Christopher. The conditions had been bitter, although the Thames had drawn short of freezing over and Christopher returned home from work each night chilled to his bones. Then he'd come across a newspaper report about the opportunities in a land so far away it could scarcely be believed. Men and women had been shipped out as convicts but recently, a few had returned from those distant shores, with great wealth – or so the newspaper had reported. Christopher's sister had married and taken their two younger sisters with her, so, he'd decided to try his hand and tap into the wealth that New South Wales offered, promising to send money to them when he could.

On arriving in Sydney Cove, he'd secured a loan and bought his boat, naming her, Hannah Elizabeth, in honour of his mother's memory.

And now, here Christopher was, in the grounds of a mansion on the outskirts of Sydney, having shaken hands on a great business deal.

"And the views from here are simply splendid," Mr Moran said with a wave of his doughy hand. The sunlight glinted off a jewelled ring on his plump finger and Christopher once again felt the surge of determination. One day, he too would wear a ring like that. Not because he liked it but because it would mean that never again would he and his sisters go hungry.

Mr Moran took a gold watch out of his pocket. "Goodness me! Is that the time! Well, Mr Randall, I fear I must cut short the tour. And I'm sure a busy man such as yourself has more productive things to do than walk around a garden."

"It has been most delightful, Mr Moran," Christopher said politely.

"Now, if you'll follow me, I'll ring for a footman to escort you to the stable..."

"No, please don't trouble yourself. I can find my own way back."

Mr Moran bade him farewell and hurried to the house, leaving Christopher to take his time, committing every detail to memory.

Sufficient money in the bank would ensure he could provide for his sisters and himself, and one day, he'd have enough to buy a grand property. His body would give out eventually. It was a race against time, but this deal would give him the advantage at long last.

With a wriggling Shadow tucked under her arm, Abigail hurried downstairs and outside into the garden where the men had been. Her father, however, was nowhere to be seen and his visitor was striding towards her on his way to the stables.

He was even more handsome than Abigail had first thought and she suddenly felt very young and foolish standing in the garden in the heat with a wriggling dog tucked under her arm. She wished she hadn't been so hasty and had taken more care with her appearance. But it was too late now. As he approached, he took off his cocked hat and bowed.

"Good day, sir. Welcome to Westervale Hall, I... I was looking for my father, Mr Moran. I believe you were with him a short while ago..." Well, that was close enough to the truth. She certainly couldn't tell this man she was trying to find out who he was.

"Good day to you, Miss Moran. I'm afraid you've missed your father. He's just returned to his study."

"Thank you, Mr...?"

"Randall," he said inclining his head again, "At your service, Miss Moran."

Randall? Had Abigail misheard his surname? She'd thought her parents had said Hanville or Granville. Perhaps they'd said, Randall. Why hadn't she paid more attention?

With alarm, she realised she was staring at him, her mind empty. If only she'd thought this through before she'd rushed into the garden. At their first meeting she should have tried to impress him, not appeared as limp as a wilted flower – and with as much to say for herself.

"I..." she started but she could think of nothing to add. Finally, she settled on, "Thank you, sir."

"Well, if you'll excuse me, Miss Moran," he said, nodding once more and attempting to move around her. As he stepped to one side, so did she – in the same direction and both stopped abruptly.

Shadow wriggled more frantically, and as she bent to set him on the ground, she imagined he'd seen a bird and would bound away to give chase. It was the perfect opportunity to hurry away after him and hide her blazing cheeks. However, to her surprise, Shadow leapt up at the man's legs, with tail wagging.

"Shadow!" Abigail called crossly, lunging for him. Catching a heel in her petticoats, she lost balance, and toppled over backwards.

Mr Randall leaned towards her and held out his hand to help her up. She wanted to scramble to her feet, pick up Shadow and rush into the house to hide her flaming cheeks but it would be the height of rudeness not to accept his offer of help, so she held out her hand. Then, realising it was her left hand and that she ought to be using her right, she retracted it and held out the other. He appeared momentarily confused as she exchanged hands but finally pulled her up, keeping hold of her until she'd regained her balance. And still, he held her hand. Did he believe she couldn't stand on her own feet? She looked up at him, wondering why he hadn't let go, but as soon as their eyes met, he released her.

Could this situation become any more embarrassing? Mercifully, he bent over and patted the dog's head. "Shadow, is it? Well, you're black enough to be a shadow, little fellow."

"I'm so sorry, Mr Randall," Abigail said, scooping the dog up into her arms.

"No harm done, Miss Moran." The corners of his mouth twitched.

She wanted to groan aloud. He was surely laughing at her. And why not? She must appear so young and unsophisticated after the ladies of London. Her curiosity and impetuosity had led her to make a silly spectacle of herself.

"Come, Shadow," she said and summoning as much dignity as she could muster, she turned and hurried back to the house.

His boots crunched on the gravel, and she knew without turning around that he was walking quickly towards the stables. If he'd had any hopes of finding a bride, she'd done nothing to persuade him he'd find one in Westervale Hall. A man as handsome as Mr Randall would have his pick of women, she was certain.

She reminded herself she didn't want to get married. But neither did she want to be rejected. If only she'd waited until he'd come to dinner and there had been proper introductions. She'd have been prepared. She wouldn't have been so tongue-tied. She wouldn't have fallen over at his feet and made such a fool of herself...

That evening at dinner, she would try to steer the conversation towards Mr Randall and find out more about him without letting her parents know she'd already met him, so it would be best if Shadow remained upstairs in her bedroom. She shook her head in disbelief at her foolishness, and dread filled her when she imagined how her father would take the news that she'd already met the suitor he'd invited to their home in the most embarrassing of circumstances.

That evening, after Molly had finished dressing her, Abigail peered into the mirror. Her hair was now pinned up, leaving golden ringlets to lightly brush the shoulders of her cornflower blue, silk gown. If only she'd looked elegant and composed like this earlier when she'd encountered Mr Randall in the garden.

While Molly had been brushing her hair, tying up laces and fastening her buttons, Abigail had been silent, trying to think of a question that would prompt either of her parents to discuss Mr Randall and his plans without arousing their suspicions. His expression was still etched on her mind. It had been a look of mild amusement, such as one might have whilst watching the antics of a foolish child but there had been something else besides. Reserve, perhaps? Or disdain? Certainly not the admiration she'd craved.

What is it to you? Abigail asked herself crossly. It's not as if you want to marry. The thought of escaping Mama's restrictions was appealing but now she knew her father had already begun marriage negotiations; the prospect had become too real... and threatening. And yet, her pride recoiled at the thought she'd not had the opportunity to win Mr Randall's regard, even if she intended to reject him. Or did she? Thoughts whirled around her brain. It was all so confusing. Once again, she wished she had someone to talk to. There was no point asking Molly. Abigail had made the mistake of taking her into her confidence a few days ago after Lottie had likened the birthmark to a dolphin.

"Hmm. some might say it's a dolphin," Molly had said studying the back of Abigail's hand, but her brows were raised in doubt. Abigail wasn't surprised. She'd noticed that although Molly was never disobedient, she had an air of insolence that always came to the fore when Abigail was uncertain and needed advice. It was subtle and cloaked in deference, but the maid usually managed to convey her greater experience and knowledge of the world with the arch of an eyebrow, the twitch of her lips or a barely perceptible snort of derision.

"And then again, others might not," Molly had said with a shrug and the ghost of a sneer. Abigail had hastily pulled her glove on, feeling unreasonable anger towards both Molly who liked to embarrass her and Lottie who'd made her hope the mark wasn't as unsightly as Mama had led her to believe.

"Is something wrong with your appearance, miss?" Molly asked, pulling Abigail out of her daydream, "Only you've been staring into that looking glass for some time."

Abigail sighed and shook her head. How she longed to ask someone about marriage and falling in love. So much so, that she wondered if it might be worth taking a chance that her maid wouldn't, once again, treat her with thinly disguised scorn.

"Do you ever think about getting married, Molly?" The words were out of her mouth before she could stop them and she cringed, waiting for her maid's derision.

But unexpectedly, Molly appeared to be rather abashed. "One day, miss. Me and Ben Armitage... well... me and Ben have an understanding. But not yet. When he gets his pardon. We'll think about it then."

Abigail was shocked. Molly and Ben Armitage, one of Father's grooms intended to marry? And she'd had no idea. She suddenly felt on the outside of something although she didn't know what – like a child peering through a window into a room full of adults.

"Why d'you ask, miss?"

"I... I was just wondering," Abigail stammered.

"I expect your father has someone in mind for you."

"Perhaps... But I'm not sure I want to marry."

"Oh, everyone wants to marry, miss." The usual Molly was back, and she looked at Abigail as if she was a child.

"So, you love Ben?" Abigail asked, ignoring her maid's reply.

Molly considered for a moment. "He's kind and he cares for me. He'll make a good father when the time comes." She occupied herself rearranging one of Abigail's ringlets, her face blank. Then spotting her

41

mistress's puzzled expression, she added tartly, "No one marries for love, miss! It's just something made up in stories."

That couldn't be true, surely? Abigail's mind spun. As she walked slowly down the stairs to the dining room, she compared the married couples she knew and the characters she'd read about in books. Mama and Papa called each other 'My love' and 'My dear' but they were nothing like Anthony and Cleopatra, Romeo and Juliet or Paris and Helen. Not, of course, that their stories had ended happily. But maybe that was the heart of the matter, couples might start by falling in love, and then it didn't last. Either death parted the lovers, or they married and slipped into a comfortable existence where they spent much of their time apart like her parents and like all the other married people she knew. Why hadn't this occurred to her before?

By the time she reached the dining room, she still had no idea how to initiate a conversation with her parents about Mr Randall without mentioning him. Her stomach churned with nerves at all the possible outcomes. If only she'd thought things through before she'd given him an opportunity to see her in a dishevelled state, trip clumsily and stutter with embarrassment. He'd be sure to tell Papa... And then Mama would start... Perhaps it was best to keep quiet and wait for the inevitable trouble.

Papa was deep in thought and chewed his food silently during dinner. Unusually, however, Mama was cheerful.

"I've received word from Mrs Hippesley that our gowns will be ready for a fitting shortly, Abigail," she said.

"Yes, Mama."

Her mother looked questioningly at Papa. "Thomas?"

"Yes, my love?"

"Have we had word yet about Mr Hanville's arrival?"

Hanville? Abigail looked at her father, expecting him to correct Mama. Earlier, the man had definitely said, Randall.

"No sign of the Pegasus yet, but I'm assured it will arrive soon."

Abigail realised she was holding her breath. She slowly released it. The man she'd met earlier was merely one of Papa's business associates or one of the governor's men. The relief! She wanted to burst out laughing. So, there was still a chance to impress her would-be suitor, and Mr Randall would have no reason to mention to Papa he'd met his daughter in the garden. It would have been of no significance to him at all.

"You're very quiet this evening, Thomas, my dear," Mama said.

"Mm? Oh, yes, sorry, my love. I've a lot on my mind. I struck an excellent business deal today."

"Oh." Mama sounded apprehensive. "Does that mean you'll be away from home for longer?"

"No. It won't take me from home at all. You know I was thinking of extending my business along the Hawkesbury River?"

Mama nodded.

"Well, I engaged the service of a young man involved in the packet trade, today, who'll be organising deliveries for me."

"But you have someone who carries your goods along the Parramatta River, why do you need someone new?"

"Ah, but the Parramatta and the Hawkesbury are two very different places," Papa said as if talking to a child, "The journey to the Hawkesbury River is dangerous and not many captains are willing to sail there regularly. It's much easier sailing up and down the Parramatta. But Mr Randall has guaranteed a service to the Hawkesbury, whatever the weather."

Abigail's appetite returned. It was unlikely she'd ever see Mr Randall again, so her earlier embarrassment could be forgotten. And Mr Hanville was still to arrive. That gave her time to think. If only she had a friend with whom she could discuss these things. Molly had been quite hesitant when she'd mentioned marriage earlier, but she'd soon resumed her usual disrespect and Abigail decided against offering herself up for further ridicule.

Then, it came to her. She'd write to Lottie in the morning and bring her back to Westervale Hall on a pretext of requesting more embroidery work. The time they'd spent together had been so enjoyable. Despite her earlier thoughts about distrusting people from the lower class, it was hard to believe Lottie was anything other than a genuinely pleasant person, and Abigail was certain she'd seen kindness and affection in her eyes.

Mama had always told her not to trust anyone in service. "They're not like us, Abigail. People from the lower classes only want to use us." Well, perhaps Mama was right but there was only one way to determine if this was true. She'd find a way of bringing Lottie back to spend time with her. And if Mama was right, then Abigail need never see Lottie again.

CHAPTER FIVE

A week later, a letter arrived at Westervale Hall for Papa. He read the contents as he was eating breakfast with his wife and daughter.

"Well, it seems the Pegasus has docked in Sydney Cove. Mr Hanville is expected to arrive later today."

"Oh!" Mama's voice trembled and she put her coffee cup down without taking a sip. "Come along, Abigail, there's no time to tarry. We have much to do."

Abigail's mouth had gone dry. She'd barely eaten anything but now she'd lost her appetite.

So, at last, she would meet Mr Hanville. But what poor timing. Abigail had arranged for Lottie to come that afternoon. She'd told Mama she had some ideas for embroidery on one of her new dresses and had asked if she could discuss them with Lottie when they went to Hippesley's Emporium again.

"I'm much too busy preparing for our guest; he could be here at any moment, you know," Mama had replied to her daughter's request.

Abigail had known. How could anyone have forgotten? But she'd nodded dutifully.

"Perhaps Lottie could come here?" Abigail had suggested as if she'd just thought of the idea and hadn't been pinning her hopes on such an outcome.

"Yes, yes!" Mama had said, waving her away irritably.

Abigail had immediately sent a message inviting Lottie to Westervale Hall, and to compensate for giving up her free afternoon, she'd ensure Lottie left with an order for some embroidery work. During that time, it would give them a chance to talk, and Abigail would surely be able to determine whether Lottie's friendliness was sincere or simply pretence in order to ingratiate herself.

And now, the eagerly awaited visit would be delayed. While Molly prepared her day clothes, Abigail wrote a letter to Lottie explaining they'd have to postpone their meeting as the family had an important guest arriving later that day. She didn't know when he'd leave but as soon as he'd gone, she'd write to Lottie again and hoped she'd be able to come to Westervale Hall.

"Please ensure that Lottie Jackson at Hippesley's Emporium gets this letter, Molly."

The maid took the letter and tucked it in her pocket.

"You won't forget, will you, Molly?"

"No, miss." Her usual scowl had returned.

Since the news had come that Mr Hanville's ship had docked and that his arrival was imminent, it seemed that everyone was distracted and irritable.

"You'd think it were the king himself who were coming," Molly grumbled as she brushed Abigail's hair.

Abigail was sympathetic. Mama was in a heightened state of frenzy. Even Papa had fled the house and sought refuge in the cool of the temple. Mr Hanville might only have been the third son of a baronet, but his visit was to be treated as if he was royalty.

Abigail felt foolish, wondering how she could possibly have thought Mr Randall had been the guest they'd all been expecting for weeks. It was more evidence – if any were needed – that she was naive. There'd been no preparations heralding Mr Randall's arrival; indeed, nothing to mark his visit at all. Hardly surprising of course, since he'd simply been Papa's business acquaintance, nevertheless, his appearance had been a useful – if somewhat embarrassing lesson. It had shown her she needed to think before acting; to curb her impetuosity. She would try to make a good impression and as for the question of marriage, she'd think about that later.

It was a shame she wouldn't see Lottie later that day as she'd have liked to find out if she had a sweetheart and... and what? Ask Lottie what she should do about Mr Hanville? Or indeed if there was anything she could do if Papa decided she should marry. Of course, not. It was absurd for the daughter of the Morans to ask for advice from a shopgirl. Or was it? Abigail had so many questions and no one to ask. It was like there was a hole in her life; the lack of something – or perhaps someone. For as long as she could remember, she'd wondered if everyone felt like that, and one day, she'd unwisely asked Molly if she felt something was missing from her life.

"A pocket full o' money, a big house and an 'andsome man," Molly had said with a laugh and Abigail had known better than to pursue the matter. For the first time, she'd realised how insensitive it might be for her – the girl with everything, to discuss a lack of anything with a girl who had nothing.

Out of the three items that Molly claimed she was lacking, Abigail had money and a fine house. But not a man. Perhaps that was what was missing from her life? But Mama had all three things. Did she feel complete? Abigail didn't think so. Mama never seemed to be satisfied, so perhaps Molly was wrong...

Abigail gasped as Molly tugged at a tangle.

"The pearls, miss?" Molly asked.

"Pearls?"

"Earrings, miss. Pearls or Jade?"

"Oh, yes, sorry, the pearls now and the jade or perhaps the diamonds later."

"And slippers," Molly said holding two pairs up for her mistress's inspection.

"Those," said Abigail pointing to the ivory slippers that matched her dress.

If only it was so easy to answer the sort of questions Abigail wanted to ask.

Once she was dressed, Molly was called to help elsewhere in the house and Abigail waited in her room, stroking Shadow, and hoping he wouldn't miss her too much when Mr Hanville arrived.

It had been over two hours since Papa had sent his carriage to the harbourside to wait for Mr Hanville and his luggage, and to convey them the short distance to Westervale Hall but when he finally arrived, Mama, Papa and Abigail were there waiting, ready to greet him.

"Really, Abigail!" Mama said as the carriage turned into the drive, "The sun is so fierce today, where is your parasol? The ivory one would have set off your outfit beautifully."

"I... I'm not sure, Mama, I believe I've mislaid it," Abigail lied. It was the one she'd lent to Lottie, but it probably wouldn't be a good idea to admit that.

"Well, it's too late to do anything about it now," Mama said.

"I'm sure he won't notice, my love," Papa said, "as soon as he arrives, we'll go inside anyway."

The house had been in such a state of anxiety all day, Abigail felt quite exhausted and not ready for the long evening ahead during which she knew she must sparkle. Dread, excitement and panic in equal measure filled her.

At last, their guest arrived and stepped down from the carriage. Abigail heard her mother emit a tiny squeak and she could see why. Mr Hugh Hanville was devastatingly handsome. Tall, slim and elegant. His blonde hair was tied back and as he approached the waiting family, a smile lit up his face; his eyes like sparkling sapphires. The colour was so intense that when he shook Abigail's hand, she found it hard to look away. He seemed equally taken with her, keeping hold of her hand for a fraction too long.

46

As Papa led them back up the steps into the cool of the house, Mama threw Abigail a triumphant look as if to place her seal of approval on their guest, followed by a slight frown and shake of her head as if she doubted her daughter's ability to win such an eligible man.

Abigail wasn't sure about marriage – that was a step beyond anything her imagination might conjure up, but she wanted to spend more time with Mr Hugh Hanville, to stare into those intriguing eyes and find out all about him.

The next few days passed in a whirl of social events – picnics, music recitals, boat trips and a dinner at the house of the new governor, Captain William Bligh. Mr Hanville was attentive to both Mrs and Miss Moran, and Abigail was amused to see her mother's cheeks flame and to hear her nervous giggle when he paid her compliments.

"He is simply charming," Mama whispered to Abigail behind her fan. "Do your best to please him." She glanced down at Abigail's hands and frowned.

However, Mr Hanville appeared to be easily pleased – he smiled readily, and his eyes sparkled in amusement with more depth of colour than the sky in the stained-glass window Papa had paid to have installed in St. Michael's Church. Wherever they went, the women fluttered and fussed around him, yet he always sought Abigail's eyes. The corners of his mouth would rise and the skin around his eyes would crinkle as if he was sending her a message that he'd rather be with her. But always, there were people with them and after a week, Abigail realised she'd hardly spoken more than a few sentences to him. At various dinners and social events, he'd asked informed questions about the problems the previous governor had encountered and his reforms, as well as how his successor, Governor Bligh was settling in. He'd regaled the guests with stories of his life in London. The plays he'd attended in the city's various theatres had sounded fascinating, as had the colonnade decorated with coloured lanterns in Vauxhall Pleasure Gardens. And shockingly, he described duels that had taken place; ghostly in Hyde Park's early morning mist. He'd refused to say whether he'd been one of the duellists but gave the impression that he had fought on various occasions. To Abigail, it all sounded so thrilling and daring. She could hardly believe he was looking for a wife with whom to share all those marvels, much less that he would choose her.

Day followed day and Mr Hanville was as gracious to the Morans, as ever, but still, he made no sign he was interested in marriage – at least, not marriage to Abigail. It was disappointing but also almost a relief. How would she cope living the sort of life Mr Hanville had described in London? She barely knew anything about Sydney. And worse, on the few occasions when Shadow had escaped from Abigail's bedroom and had spotted Mr Hanville, he'd growled, baring his teeth. Abigail had been appalled. She'd scooped the dog up and chided him as she'd carried him back to her bedroom. It was evident Shadow had taken a dislike to Mr Hanville, and he, in turn, made it clear the feeling was mutual. If she married him, she knew she'd have to leave Shadow behind and that in all likelihood, Mama would turn him out of Westervale Hall.

As the date of Mr Hanville's departure approached, Mama became increasingly agitated at his lack of declaration. Abigail knew she constantly questioned Papa to find out if he knew more. It wasn't until the eve of his departure that Abigail, who was at the top of the stairs coming down for dinner, caught sight of Mr Hanville entering her father's study. She went down to the dining room where Mama was pacing excitedly and several minutes later, she was summoned to the study, where Papa and Mr Hanville were waiting for her – both men smiling with satisfaction.

"Ah, Abigail, my dear, please come in. I shall leave you with Mr Hanville to tell you the exciting news."

Abigail's parents were in the entrance hall. She could hear them whispering until her father closed the study door leaving her alone with Mr Hanville.

"I've just asked your father for your hand in marriage, Miss Moran." He beamed at her delightedly. "And under the circumstances, perhaps you will now permit me to call you, Abigail?"

"Yes," she said breathlessly and then realised he'd taken her agreement for him to use her Christian name as her acceptance of his proposal. Although, she mused, he hadn't actually asked her to marry him. But it was still a proposal of marriage, wasn't it? She had so many questions. When would they marry? When would they leave for London? Would he allow time for Shadow to become accustomed to him?

"Excellent. And you must call me Hugh now we're to be married."

Married? She was promised to be married? It was as easy as that? "W... when will we marry?" she stammered, having a flashback to the time a snake had startled the horse and it had bolted, dragging the carriage after it. Everything was going too fast.

"No need to worry your pretty head about that," Hugh said, "I'll arrange a time with your father. But not for a few weeks. I'll be staying in town for a while. I have affairs to attend to."

"Where will we marry?" she asked.

"I'll leave that to your father to arrange."

"And will we live in London?"

"My, my! So many questions! I hope this is merely excitement and not an indication that you are unable to curb your curiosity."

She gasped with surprise at his sharp tone. Surely, he hadn't been serious? But his brows were drawn together in an angry line suggesting that he had. Beneath them, his eyes had turned an icy blue – and they appeared to be just as cold.

It must be the light, she told herself. His eyes were so remarkable, they changed hue with the light. It was nothing more.

He held out his arm to her, and his smile that had once been so warm, now seemed merely a movement of his lips. "Well, Abigail, let's go to dinner, shall we? I have such an appetite this evening."

Abigail had to remind herself that on a date that was still to be arranged, she would walk down the aisle with her father, to wed the stranger who was now cutting into the crust of the meat pie on his plate opposite her. She chewed her food and tried to swallow but it was as if she was eating sawdust.

Mama trilled like the colourful birds that filled the trees in Westervale Hall's orchards and Papa laughed heartily at everything Hugh said. And her future husband smiled with his blue eyes twinkling, once again like the stained-glass sky in St. Michael's Church where it was possible, they would take their vows.

A dinner party was planned to celebrate the coming marriage and of course, there would be a lavish wedding on some date still to be agreed, but by the time Abigail and her mother retired to the withdrawing room, leaving the men to their brandy, she still didn't know where the newly married couple would eventually live. Hugh had mentioned his father's house in Grosvenor Square, London and an estate in Yorkshire but hadn't said whether either place would be their home or indeed if they would leave for England at all.

Mama seemed to have heard what she wanted to hear, and she clasped her hands together. "There's so much to prepare! We must have new gowns fit for London."

Abigail remained silent. 'We must have new gowns' – who was Mama referring to when she said 'we'? If they went to England, would Mama

49

accompany them? The situation was like a rock rolling downhill, gathering speed. It would be senseless to get in its way.

"I shall write to Mrs Greenway. She has three married daughters and will be able to guide us." Mama turned her head this way and that as if she didn't know what to do first. "After Mr Han... or should I say Hugh departs tomorrow, we'll go into town and see Mrs Hippesley. She'll know what the best-dressed brides are wearing." Mama paused. "Oh, and by the way, Molly tells me that girl who came here from the Emporium to deliver your gloves, took your parasol. I shall have a word with Mrs Hippesley about that."

"No!" Abigail said, "Lottie didn't take it, I lent it to her. She was feeling faint, and the day was so hot, I thought it would keep the sun off her a little. But she'll have it ready for me the next time I see her."

"Of course, I didn't think she stole it, Abigail. That's not what I said. But she should have known better than to take it... even if you offered to lend it to her. Goodness knows what you were thinking to have done that! If I've told you once, I've told you a hundred times, there is a certain way to treat servants and those of the lower classes. It doesn't do to be over-friendly. It gives them ideas above their station and before you know it, they're taking advantage of you."

"But she wasn't taking advantage of me, she wasn't well—"

"People of that class are much stronger than they appear." Mama sniffed. "They're used to working hard. It isn't wise to over-indulge them."

"But she does work hard, Mama, and she's all alone."

"You seem to know a lot about this shopgirl, Abigail."

"No, not at all!" Appealing to her mother's kinder instinct was obviously not working. Abigail tried another tack. "Her work is excellent," she said holding out her gloved hands so Mama could see the colourful butterflies.

"Yes," Mama admitted, inspecting the gloves, "she is skilful."

"I... I wondered if we could insist she worked on everything we need before the wedding. She's had such a sad life."

Mama frowned at Abigail. "She told you about her life? How long was she here?"

"Not long and she only explained some of the things in the sampler that relate to her life—"

"Sampler? What sampler? I didn't pay for a sampler! Honestly Abigail sometimes I think you believe your father plucks money from the trees!"

"No, it was a gift. Father didn't pay for it."

"A gift? Why ever would she send a gift? Good gracious, girl! Haven't I told you how the lower classes will try to gain favour for their own ends? You must ignore them. Convicts, emancipists, anyone who associates with that class of person. They're all dishonest! You cannot trust them. Show me this gift, we shall return it tomorrow."

"No! Please, Mama!"

"Bring it here, at once!"

Abigail sighed. She was tempted to refuse but surely, once Mama saw the delicacy of the stitches, she would realise Lottie's worth. It wasn't like Papa had paid for it. And anyway, tonight was not the time to argue while Hugh was still in the house. He may have shaken hands with Papa, but at this stage, the marriage proposal was still so new, Abigail wasn't sure if it could easily be retracted. For a second, she considered that would be a good thing and then suppressed the thought. Once she was in London or Yorkshire or wherever Hugh took her, she'd be mistress of her own house and she'd have samplers made by whomever she chose. And she would do as she liked... And if Mama accompanied them to England, she'd return eventually. She wouldn't be able to stay away from Papa and their home for long.

On the morrow, after Hugh had left, Abigail would insist on keeping the sampler, even if it meant she had to hide it away from Mama.

"Fetch it now," her mother said. Abigail rose and ran upstairs to get the sampler.

"See how exquisitely it's been done, Mama," Abigail said on her return, "Those waves almost appear to be real."

"What nonsense! This is no better than any other work I've seen. And what is the point of it anyway?"

"It's a nature scene," Abigail said, reluctant to explain about the dolphin.

"And yet, she felt the need to explain parts of this scene by telling you about her life?" Mama asked and Abigail swallowed nervously.

"So which parts of this relate to the girl's history? I expect the ship represents the one on which she arrived? A convict transport ship?"

"Yes, but she's not a convict, she came with her mother."

"Ha! The daughter of a convict!"

"She can't help who her mother was. But she's working honestly and making the best of it. She was only three when she arrived."

"I expect the woman brought a whole brood of children and they've been living off the Governor's stores ever since."

"Her mother died when Lottie was very young and so did her baby

51

sister, so, no, there is no brood in Sydney, just Lottie. See here." Abigail drew her mother's attention back to the sampler. "Lottie embroidered their initials so cleverly amongst the foliage. Here's M.J. for Mary Jackson, her mother, and here are her initials, C.J. and here is A.J. for baby Amelia, who died a few days after she was born."

Mama took a deep breath, and it was a second or two before Abigail realised she hadn't breathed out. She sat like a statue staring at the sampler the only sign of life were large beads of sweat popping out on her brow and a vein pulsing in her temple.

"Mama?" Abigail asked anxiously, "Are you ill?"

But there was no reply. Her mother released her breath. It came out in short sharp gasps and her face looked waxy.

"Fetch your father, Abigail!" she said through clenched teeth.

Abigail ran for Papa and knocked timidly on the dining room door.

After that, servants were called, Mama was carried upstairs to her bedroom and the doctor was summoned. It wasn't until the following morning Abigail realised someone had tidied away the sampler although none of the servants knew where it was and claimed not to have seen it.

The following morning Abigail waited at the front of the house with Papa, his eyes dark from lack of sleep, to wish Hugh godspeed on his trip to Parramatta. Hugh had told the Morans he had some business to attend to and once that was concluded, he'd return to Sydney. He'd said he'd stay in a hotel rather than inconvenience Mrs Moran, despite his host's assurances that his wife would be better by then. Hugh promised to send word on his return to town and shaking hands with Mr Moran, he turned to Abigail who thought he was going to shake hers. However, he took her hand and lifted it to his lips, his smile and sky-blue eyes taking her breath away, but as he let go of her hand and turned away, she thought – or perhaps imagined – that the smile had lost its warmth and become a mere lift of the corners of his mouth and his eyes were once again ice-cold chips. His last glance as the carriage set off did not seek out her face, it appeared to be taking in the entire mansion. Or was she imagining it?

Immediately after Hugh left, Papa called for a horse to be saddled so he could ride to town. Abigail wondered if Hugh had left something behind that Papa intended to return. While he was gone, Abigail offered to read to Mama, but she said she'd rather be left alone to rest as the doctor had advised, so after surreptitiously searching for the sampler, Abigail went back to her bedroom. Sitting on the window seat, Abigail saw Papa return several hours later, his face haggard. Poor Papa, he was so anxious about Mama.

After two days, Mama had still not regained her strength. The doctor had visited several times and Papa had spent hours in her room talking to her in a low voice. Abigail wondered if Papa was reading to her although from time to time, Mama's voice could be heard too – a muffled, high-pitched sound as if she was crying.

Had Abigail been the cause of her mother's condition? She'd simply told the truth. How could that be wrong? No, it couldn't have been her fault... Perhaps her mother's decline was merely a coincidence.

When Abigail awoke the following morning, Mama was still in bed and Papa had left word that he was going to town and would return before evening. Another lonely, tedious day stretched before her. How she longed to see a friendly face. She considered sending a message to see if Lottie could come to Westervale Hall. Mama need never find out. They could meet in the temple. Abigail would persuade Cook to make a picnic.

Don't be so foolish! she told herself. Of course, Lottie wouldn't be able to come – she'd be at work. However, suppose Abigail went to visit Lottie? Why not? She could order the carriage to take her and Molly into town and they could visit Hippesley's Emporium. Lottie would be there and at least if they couldn't talk, Abigail would spend some time with her. Yes, it was perfect!

Abigail informed Molly that after she'd helped her to dress, she'd accompany her to town so they could check on the progress of the gowns.

"There ain't no hurry, miss. The master won't allow a wedding to take place while Mistress is poorly. So, it's not like you can make any decisions until she's well."

"I... I simply want to see what they look like so far," Abigail said. She didn't sound convincing and although she didn't need to justify herself to Molly, she added, "The truth is, I lent my parasol to Lottie Jackson, and I wish to retrieve it. And, by the by, why did you tell Mama I'd lent it to her?"

"Because when the mistress asked you about it, you said you'd mislaid it and she blamed me for being untidy. So, I told her the girl had it," Molly said, her mouth set in a sulky line. "I'm not getting into trouble for no thieving shopgirl and that's the truth."

"But I explained to Mama I'd lent it to Lottie."

"Well, Mistress believes the girl stole it. And so does Master."

"Papa?" Why was Papa interested in something he would normally describe as women's trifles? A feeling of dread pressed down in her stomach like a stone.

Molly shrugged. "He's not likely to explain himself to me, I'm sure."

"I don't understand! I told Mama I'd lent it to Lottie and explained why," Abigail said tying the ribbon garter over one stocking just above her knee, "I was most clear." She tugged hard at the bow.

"Well, perhaps Mistress's sickness drove it from her mind," said Molly handing her the other stocking.

Abigail was silent as she rolled it up her leg. "Perhaps... Anyway, how do you know what my parents think about Lottie?" The stone grew harder and heavier inside her.

"Because when I was in Mistress's room tidying up, I overheard their conversation."

"Tell me exactly what was said."

"No, I shouldn't do that, Miss Abigail."

But Abigail knew she would. Molly couldn't help showing how much more she knew than her young mistress.

"Well, they were both angry that Lottie had been here, and Mistress said that Master had to do something about it."

"Do something? Such as?" Abigail's voice became shrill.

"I don't know. She sent me from the room, so I didn't hear no more. But I know she's already written to Mrs Hippesley. And Master's been to see her."

"Papa's been to see Mrs Hippesley?" Abigail's hand flew to her mouth. "Why?" she whispered.

"I don't know," Molly said airily, "to tell her Lottie stole the parasol? Perhaps to get it back?"

"Then where is it?"

"I don't know!" Molly scowled, holding her hands palm upwards as if she wanted nothing to do with the parasol.

"This is simply dreadful!" Abigail wailed, and for once Molly looked at her with sympathy.

"Why do you care?" The maid looked at her in surprise.

Why *did* Abigail care? Well, because somehow, her attempt at kindness had resulted in this confusion and an innocent girl had been accused of theft. It was bad enough that Abigail was responsible, but it was even worse that she liked Lottie. She might only be a shopgirl and the daughter of a convict but for some reason, it mattered deeply. What would Mrs Hippesley do about Papa's allegations? Surely, she wouldn't dismiss her best seamstress. Lottie had told Abigail that as well as being her employer, Mrs Hippesley was one of the women who'd looked after her, so she'd know Lottie wouldn't have stolen a parasol. And yet any of her girls who visited a rich client's house and appeared with something such as a parasol might fall under suspicion. Despite what Mama had said initially, she didn't believe Abigail had lent it to her, so why would Mrs Hippesley?

Abigail would not go into town now – she dared not risk making things worse for Lottie. But as soon as Papa returned, Abigail would explain everything to him and make sure he understood that Mama had been mistaken. That would put everything right.

When Abigail thought about it later, she realised she'd been too agitated and emotional when she'd burst into Papa's library that afternoon on his return. Why hadn't she rehearsed her words? She'd certainly had sufficient time during the hours she'd spent alone to prepare a speech. But as soon as she started speaking, Papa's face had hardened, and instead of trying to win him over, she'd raised her voice. The result had been that not only had Papa ignored her claim that the parasol hadn't been stolen but he'd been unusually harsh and when, in desperation, Abigail had threatened to go to see Mrs Hippesley and tell her the truth, he'd ordered her to go to her room and stay there. She would not be allowed the freedom to go out, with or without Molly, and she would remain home until Hugh returned and a decision was made about the wedding date. After that, he said she'd be her husband's property and she'd have to do as he told her. But while she was under her father's roof, she'd do as he said.

Abigail bit back angry, bitter words, shocked at her father's unfairness, but she'd returned to her bedroom where she'd hugged Shadow and sobbed. Why was her kind, gentle father acting like this? Of course, he was worried about Mama and still spent more time than usual with her, but she was gradually improving, according to Molly, so why was Papa still so enraged? And why direct his anger at Lottie?

However, if Papa had become harder, then strangely, Molly had become kinder. She brought Abigail a few biscuits to make up for missing supper.

"Not to worry, miss. Lottie's gone now, and your Mama seems to be a bit better. I'll wager she'll be up tomorrow."

"Lottie's gone? Gone where?"

Molly shrugged. "Master told Mistress she's gone. That's all I know."

Once the maid had left, Shadow, seeming to feel his mistress's agitation, stirred, scratched his ear and looked up adoringly.

"I can't seem to do anything without hurting someone," she said bending over to tickle his chin, "Lottie's gone and Mama's sick – and somehow, I think it's all because of me. What can I do Shadow?" she asked, but of course, there was no reply

The following morning, Mama was well enough to leave her bedroom for a light breakfast and Abigail wondered if things would start to get back to normal. She left Shadow in her bedroom and joined her parents, dreading spending time with them, not only because she expected their disapproval but because she was burning with resentment that she knew she must conceal.

"Your father tells me Hugh is in Parramatta," Mama said, "and since it may be several weeks before he's back and we can set a wedding date, I will arrange for Mrs Hippesley to come here with samples of fabrics, styles and, of course, to do our fittings."

"But—" However Abigail didn't finish her objection, as both parents turned on her at once.

"For once, Abigail, do as you are told!" Mama said.

"Yes! Take heed of your mother!" Papa's face was cold and hard.

The meal continued in silence and Abigail was grateful when it finished, and she could return to Shadow.

Abigail bristled at her parents' unfairness. It seemed she couldn't do anything right. She considered taking her sketching things to the temple, but she couldn't summon the enthusiasm. However, as dull as her day promised to be, she couldn't help wondering about Lottie. Where was she waking up? And how would she fill her hours?

Shadow scratched at the door and Abigail fetched his leash. She reflected that she had as much control over her life as the dog had over his – unable to come and go as she pleased. Anger and frustration bubbled up inside. Thank goodness she'd only be confined to the house until Hugh returned. Once he was back, they could set a date and then she'd be mistress of her own world. But until then she had to do as her parents said... Or did she? Suppose she took things into her own hands and secretly left Westervale Hall? She could escape long enough to go to Sydney and find out where Lottie was. What could Mama and Papa do? They could lock her in her bedroom, of course, but only after she'd returned. And as soon as Hugh came, they'd have to let her out.

Abigail tugged on the bellpull and by the time Molly appeared, Abigail had a plan to find out where Lottie was. Unfortunately, she'd need to take Molly into her confidence and trust her, but there was no choice – she couldn't act alone. It was quite straightforward. She'd walk into Sydney and go to see Mrs Hippesley to find out what had happened.

"First, I need a set of clothes such as a servant would wear," Abigail said. She'd be less noticeable if she was dressed plainly.

"You're going to dress up like a servant?" Molly laughed. "Mrs Hippesley will recognise you whatever you're wearing, and she'll be afraid of losing your mother's custom. She'll never talk to you. And if she won't talk to you, how are you going to find Lottie?"

"I'll ask one of her girls." Abigail tossed her head, cross with herself for not realising that Molly was right.

"All of Mrs Hippesley's girls will likely know it's because of you that Lottie lost her job. No one's going to want to have anything to do with you unless you appear with your mother, and they 'ave to serve you. Turning up dressed as a servant isn't going to make them trust you any the more."

"Then what can I do?" Abigail's voice rose in anguish.

"Hush!" said Molly, "there may be a way. I have errands to run today and could keep my ears and eyes open when I go to town."

"You could?" Abigail's face was alight with hope. "I'm sure one of the girls would talk to you."

"I'm not talking to no one!" Molly said quickly, "All I said was that I'd keep my ears and eyes open. If Mistress found out I'd been asking after Lottie, I'd likely lose my position too."

"Molly, please!"

Molly thought for a moment. "I'd be taking a risk, so you'd have to make it worth my while."

"Yes, what would you like?"

"Money, of course," said Molly.

"But I don't have money! Papa pays for everything I need."

Molly shrugged.

Abigail rummaged in her jewellery box and found her jade earrings.

"If you sell these for me, I shall give you ten shillings."

Molly's eyes were fixed on the earrings and Abigail moved closer, raising her hand so they caught the light.

"These are worth a lot of money," said Abigail. She held her breath and when Molly didn't refuse, she added, "once you and Ben are married this money will be very useful..."

The maid nibbled her lower lip, unable to take her eyes off the earrings.

"All right! I'll do it," Molly said.

With a sigh of relief, Abigail held them out to her.

"No! I won't take them now. I don't want to risk having them in my pocket in case they're discovered. Look what happened to Lottie Jackson and your parasol. Who'd believe you gave them to me?"

"But I would speak up for you and admit to my plan if you were caught," said Abigail.

Molly snorted, her eyes rolling to the ceiling.

"Don't you trust me?" Abigail asked, stung at the girl's reaction.

"I don't trust no one but I particularly don't trust your ability to get me out of trouble."

"Then, I shall leave them next to the ewer on the washstand. You can take them just before you go to town."

Molly nodded her agreement.

"But what about clothes? Will you be able to bring me some?" Abigail asked looking at Molly and trying to assess how much shorter she was than the maid.

"No point eyeing up my clothes, miss," Molly said, "other than what I'm standin' up in, I've only got my Sunday best. I don't have lots of gowns like you. Anyway, why d'you need to dress up like a servant? I'm going to find out what happened to Lottie."

"But when you find out where she is, I want to go and see her."

"You'll be the last person she wants to see, miss. Trust me."

"I have to make it up to her."

Molly frowned and sniffed. "Seems to me, if I were in trouble, I don't think you'd spend any time looking for me. What's so special about Lottie Jackson?"

"I... I don't know," Abigail admitted. She certainly didn't want to explain to Molly that she'd felt some sort of connection with Lottie as if they'd known each other for years. It didn't make sense but during the time they'd spent together, Abigail had never felt more comfortable.

"Them earrings should fetch a good price and I'm sure I'll find some second-hand clothes for you in town," Molly said.

"Second-hand?" Abigail's nose wrinkled in disgust.

"Of course," said Molly nastily, "d'you want to look like a servant or d'you want people to see you're a spoiled, rich girl dressing up?"

"Yes, thank you." Abigail kept her voice level. Molly was enjoying having the upper hand but the thought of wearing somebody else's clothes made Abigail's skin itch. However, she wouldn't be able to help

58

Lottie without Molly's assistance, and this wasn't a world that Abigail knew anything about.

"An' you'll definitely give me ten shillings?"

Abigail assured her she would. She suspected Molly's pride would push her to get a good price for the earrings, so, there would be money left over and Abigail planned to give it to Lottie – however much that might be

Whilst Molly was dressing Abigail for dinner that evening, she reported what she'd discovered when she'd been in town. "I spoke to Nell, and she said Lottie has definitely gone."

"Nell?"

"Yes. Nell." Molly's eyes rolled to the ceiling. "She works for Mrs Hippesley. Don't you remember she brought Lottie when you said you wanted your gloves embroidered?"

"Yes, yes," Abigail said quickly, feeling ashamed she hadn't remembered the girl who'd served them. How had she previously been so unaware of the life and people around her?

But Molly's irritation hadn't lasted long. She had a story to tell, and she was going to be heard. "Well, Nell said your father visited Mrs Hippesley and while he was there, Lottie was called into the office. She came out crying and told Nell that Mr Moran had accused her of theft. She'd tried to return the parasol, but he'd just said that was all the proof he needed that she'd stolen it and said he intended to call a constable. Then he said he might be prepared to overlook the crime if Lottie agreed to go away. He told her he had a customer who needed a servant and he'd be prepared to drop the charges if she agreed to take the post immediately."

"So, where is Lottie now?" Abigail's mind whirled. It seemed so petty to take Lottie from her place of work and insist she became somebody's servant.

Molly shrugged. "All I know is, she's going to one of your father's customers who's settled on the banks of the Hawkesbury River."

"The Hawkes..." The word caught in Abigail's throat. She'd imagined she'd be able to find a way to visit Lottie and eventually, to rescue her but the Hawkesbury River was miles away and after Mr Randall had visited the house, Papa had mentioned how difficult it was to get there. How long ago that seemed.

"Stop!" Abigail said, pushing Molly's hands away from the laces of her stays, "I simply can't go downstairs to dinner this evening. I won't be able to hide that something is amiss. Please tell my parents I have a headache and have gone back to bed. I need time to think!"

"Yes, miss." Molly glared and rolled her eyes to the ceiling as she undid the stays she'd just laced up.

Abigail lay awake until the sun rose the following morning, puzzling about what to do. She could recite the dates of past kings and queens, she knew how to conjugate Latin verbs and how to identify animals from around the world, but she understood very little about Sydney and the people who lived in it. Of course, she knew the people of Sydney society, but not the real people who lived and worked and presumably died without her ever knowing of their existence. For someone who was so well-educated, she felt remarkably ignorant about life.

She was too tired to go to breakfast, having fallen into a fitful sleep shortly before Molly came to open her curtains and help her to dress. However, her decision to avoid supper and then breakfast prompted Mama to visit and insist she stay in bed for the day. If Abigail didn't remain in bed, Mama said, she'd send for the doctor and indeed, she was tempted to do so, anyway. Abigail agreed and assured her mother she'd be better when she'd had a chance to sleep.

Sleep? How could she sleep knowing Lottie was paying for something she hadn't done, having been banished to somewhere along the banks of the Hawkesbury River?

A tiny voice inside Abigail said, *Let it go. She's a shopgirl and nothing to you.* It could so easily have been her mother speaking and until a short while ago, it might have been Abigail's opinion too. But having met Lottie, something had changed inside her.

Nonsense, the small voice said, *you barely know the girl, she's of no importance.* But if Lottie had no value, then it seemed that Abigail's life was meaningless too.

She placed her hands on her forehead to see if it was hot. Perhaps her feigned illness hadn't been pretence at all, perhaps she really was feverish. But her forehead was cool, and her heart was beating steadily and strongly. No, she was in her right mind – and probably more so than ever before. She would somehow find out what had happened to Lottie and do something to help her.

The following day, Abigail made herself get up and behave as normally as she could, fearing her mother might send for the doctor. However, now Mama was well, she was preoccupied with inviting a succession of guests to Westervale Hall. As soon as Hugh returned, she planned to throw a lavish dinner party to announce Hugh and Abigail's engagement. But before that, she couldn't resist sharing the good news with the other members of Sydney society.

"Mr Hanville is so handsome," said Miss Anne Ferguson, who'd come with her mother and sister to Westervale Hall. She was the elder daughter of one of the senior officers of the New South Wales Corps, and she'd always made it clear she thought Abigail, as the daughter of a businessman – even an extremely wealthy businessman – was beneath her.

"How very fortunate you are, my dear," she said patting Abigail's hand. She was a year older than Abigail and the two girls had met occasionally at social gatherings but had never been friends. Now, despite the sugary words, it was obvious Anne thought it grossly unfair Abigail would be married before her.

"And he comes from London!" trilled Anne's younger – and kinder sister, Louisa, she held her hands together in delight. "How simply marvellous! How lucky you are, Miss Moran!"

Her sister glared at her but Louisa either hadn't noticed or chose to ignore her. "I long to go to London," she said, "Simply nothing happens here in Sydney."

Abigail glanced at the clock, willing the hands to turn faster. She was under no illusion that anyone was genuinely pleased for her; the unmarried girls envied her, and their mothers begrudged her such good fortune. However, it appeared that Mama was basking in the glory as the mother of the soon-to-be bride of the son of a baronet. Abigail knew she'd always been resentful that she was on the fringes of society despite Papa's fortune. Somehow, her father mixed with everyone of quality and had been accepted as one of them, but the womenfolk were more discriminating about who they admitted into their ranks and Mama felt as though she was merely tolerated.

Abigail had been instructed to tell anyone who asked that she knew nothing about her grandparents except that they had all lived in England but had died before she'd been born. Whether they were still alive or not, Abigail didn't know but she suspected both sets of grandparents had not been landed gentry as Mama claimed.

"I hope the weather will be more clement for your wedding day than it was when Isabella Rowe and Samuel Thornton married," Louisa said, "It simply poured all day. It was frightful. And there was a terrific thunderclap during their vows."

"Mama said Isabella should have listened to God's warning," Anne said, lowering her voice and casting a wary glance at the older women who were sitting on the other side of the room.

"What do you mean?" Abigail was intrigued.

"Well," Anne lowered her voice further and leaned towards the other girls. "A week after the wedding, it was discovered Samuel already had a woman and three children."

"No!" Louisa said, placing her hand over her mouth.

"Hush!" Anne said.

"But you must be wrong, Anne. He wouldn't be allowed to have two wives." Louisa shook her head emphatically.

"I didn't say he had a wife, I said he had a woman. A servant girl. They weren't married but she'd had three of his children."

"No! What did Isabella do?"

"Why, she did nothing. What could she do? She's Mrs Thornton now. The other woman doesn't have a name."

"But the children...?" Louisa's mouth hung wide open in shock.

"Three boys and they're all the image of their father, apparently. Of course, they won't inherit a farthing. And Isabella is now with child. Her son or daughter will have their father's name."

Abigail listened to the conversation, fascinated. She knew from Molly that often those of the lower classes didn't bother to marry or keep to one partner, however, she'd never heard of someone of her social standing having a family with a serving girl. But then, it wasn't often that girls of her social standing shared gossip with her.

The whispers and quiet gasps had attracted Mrs Ferguson's attention.

"And when will the dashing Mr Hanville be returning, Miss Moran?" she asked, her cold eyes sliding back and forth between her two unmarried daughters and Abigail as if she'd guessed they were gossiping. Mama cut in and explained that Mr Hanville was away on business and would return shortly to set the date and claim his bride.

"Good gracious!" Mrs Ferguson exclaimed, "is that the time? We really must be going. Come along, girls." She settled her teacup back on its saucer. "Well, my dear, this has been so pleasant we really must do it again."

Turning to Abigail, she added, "And perhaps you and Mr Hanville will call as soon as convenient. We would, of course, welcome members of Mr Hanville's family or friends – or even business acquaintances who may come to Sydney for the wedding."

The catch in her voice told Abigail that it had dented her pride to include business associates in her list of acceptable guests and it was a measure of her desperation at still having two unmarried daughters.

Mrs Ferguson was related to a duke, and she didn't approve of commerce but with two unmarried daughters, and a lack of suitable young men in Sydney, needs must.

"There was a very handsome gentleman who arrived at the same time as us, today," she said, "I wondered if perhaps he was going to join us." Mrs Ferguson's voice was regretful.

"A handsome gentleman?" Mama tapped her chin thoughtfully.

"Yes, a dark-haired man. Exceedingly good-looking..."

"Oh!" said Mama "I believe my husband has a business meeting with a gentleman who runs a packet service to the Hawkesbury."

At the mention of the Hawkesbury, Abigail held her breath. During the last few days of social events, the memory of Lottie had begun to fade. She could barely leave the house without her parents' permission, so getting to the distant reaches of the Hawkesbury to find Lottie, would only be possible if she were able to sprout wings and fly.

The little voice inside her head that echoed Mama's words, had salved her conscience. It wasn't as though Lottie had been sent away to somewhere dreadful like Norfolk Island, she'd simply moved to another place with another employer. Increasingly, people were moving to the Hawkesbury River and although occasionally there were reports of the natives rising up and attacking settlers and their farms, everyone knew it was a place of great opportunity. Perhaps it had been a good move for Lottie. Perhaps she was happier where she was. And after all, she was no one to Abigail. Simply someone she'd met and whose company she'd enjoyed. And there was so much for Abigail to think about with her wedding to plan and then the possibility of a long voyage overseas. Indeed, there was so much to think about that the small voice had become the overriding voice, convincing her that there was nothing missing from her life. There was too much to look forward to for her to worry about something over which she had no control.

A footman led Mrs and the Misses Ferguson out and Abigail accompanied them. Anne was reminding her they'd always been firm friends and she hoped Abigail would remember that and introduce her to any of her husband's family or friends at the wedding. "But of course, we've been friends for so long, Abigail dear, I know I hardly need ask you, do I?"

Abigail wanted to shake Anne's hand off her arm. But she smiled and assured her she would remember. She felt sorry for the older girl even though she'd snubbed her on more than one occasion.

Abigail waited at the top of the stone steps beneath the portico to wave to them as their carriage set off down the drive. As she turned back, a footman brought Mr Randall to the door and once he was outside, not having seen Abigail behind the pillar, the footman closed the door.

"Miss Moran," Mr Randall said with a smile. He raised his hat. "How delightful to see you again."

"Mr Randall." She blushed, remembering how foolish she'd appeared at their last meeting.

Christopher had wondered if he'd see Miss Moran again. After his last visit to Westervale Hall, her face had often appeared in his mind, and he'd made a determined effort to push it to one side so he could concentrate on his work. He'd never met anyone like her. She was young and pretty like countless other girls he'd known but she hadn't flirted like some, nor treated him with disdain and then coy glances like others. There'd been a freshness about her like a meadow full of summer flowers; unspoilt and without artfulness. The blush on her porcelain cheeks had been natural, not the result of make-up such as he'd seen on so many rich women both in Sydney and London. Her hair had escaped from beneath her bonnet, leaving tendrils that curled around her ears and forehead, and had obviously not been pinned so severely into place, they no longer resembled hair at all. Young, but no longer a child...

Stop! He told himself, recognising the familiar pattern of his thoughts, obviously brought on by being in her home. It was senseless to think of her. First, she was the daughter of a rich man who'd doubtless have plans for an advantageous match and secondly – and so much more importantly – he'd sworn never to marry. How could he help his sisters back in England and save enough to climb in society if he had a wife and family? Countless girls had offered themselves to him – some wanting no more than a night of pleasure, others wishing for a man with whom to make a home, but they'd all been disappointed – well, most of them, anyway. He'd learned his lesson in London. It was amazing how the girl who'd been so alluring at first had become demanding and manipulative, eventually stealing his savings and running away with the man who'd been her real lover. Never again. There was no time nor energy for anything but work. He neither wanted nor needed a wife and he knew Miss Moran was not someone to trifle with.

Forget her!

And then, just as he'd finished his meeting with a very satisfied Mr

Moran and had been escorted to the front door by a footman, there she was on the steps, waving goodbye to three women who'd just climbed into a carriage and were pulling away.

He bowed politely and noticed the flush rise to her cheeks. The slight frown that had previously furrowed her brow was replaced by confusion possibly because she'd heard the front door close, leaving her outside. Or perhaps she was nervous in his company. He didn't want to unsettle her – not in her own home, and he wondered if he might put her at her ease.

You fool! She'll be perfectly at ease when you leave. So, go. Leave now! You've come too far in your business plans to jeopardise them by risking angering Mr Moran who could appear at any moment. Bid her farewell immediately and continue down the steps to meet the groom who's coming with your horse.

But Christopher's feet weren't obeying the message from his brain, and he lingered.

"Mr Randall, I wonder if I may have a word with you, please?" Miss Moran said taking a step towards him.

No, his internal voice said. *Tell her you must leave. Tell her now!*

"Certainly, Miss Moran, it will be a pleasure."

"I... I understand you sail to the Hawkesbury River." She glanced nervously at the closed front doors.

"That is correct." Well, he hadn't expected that. What interest could she have in the Hawkesbury River?

"Recently, I understand that my father sent a girl somewhere along the Hawkesbury and I'm keen to have news of her."

"I see." He spoke slowly, giving himself time to think. Was this a trap? Her father had given him instructions to deliver a girl to one of the homesteads along the furthest tributary and had then sworn Christopher to secrecy. So now, he should deny all knowledge of the girl.

"Please forgive me, Miss Moran, but perhaps the best person to ask would be your father?"

Her cheeks flushed a deeper red and her mouth opened, but no words came out. Finally, she composed herself. "I believe you're correct, Mr Randall, but the truth is, I cannot. Neither can I explain why I do not wish to ask my father, but I would be willing to pay you. I... I don't have a great deal of money, but I could give you a ring to sell."

He was silent for a second. If she was acting on her father's instructions in order to trip him up, her behaviour and offer were most unusual. Indeed, she seemed close to tears. What significance was one serving girl anyway? This was a harsh, unforgiving country. People disappeared all the time.

The groom was now waiting at the bottom of the steps, and Christopher knew he shouldn't tarry – if someone should be looking from one of the windows, they'd see he hadn't claimed his horse and would wonder where he'd gone. Although they weren't overlooked, as soon as someone opened one of the front doors, he and Miss Moran would be in full view.

"Who is the girl you seek?" he asked.

"Her name is Lottie Jackson. She was a seamstress who worked in Hippesley's Emporium. I lent her a parasol but although I've explained she simply borrowed it, neither of my parents believe me, and as a result, she's been sent away. I want to find out where she is, and I want to help her."

"She must be someone special to you?"

"I... I don't know... it's hard to explain." She looked away in embarrassment and at that second, as her gaze broke from his and her eyes glanced away, he was reminded of the girl he'd conveyed on his boat. True, her eyes had been red-rimmed and full of tears, but something about Miss Moran reminded him of the girl he'd left on the banks of the Hawkesbury. He blinked as if to clear his eyes but as she looked back at him, he saw the likeness again. Different faces, different hair and he would guess, different ages and yet there was a similarity.

"There's something reminiscent of her face in yours," he said and then realised his mistake.

"So, you have seen her!" Miss Moran's hand flew to cover her mouth. The butterfly embroidered on her glove appeared to have alighted over her lips and above that, her eyes were wide with shock. For several seconds they stared at each other – he, wondering whether she'd tell her father and she...? What was she wondering? He couldn't guess what was on her mind. Shock? Joy? It was hard to tell but when she spoke, he thought her voice was full of hope.

"So, you've seen Lottie?"

Well, it was senseless now to deny he'd seen her. He nodded.

"Where did you take her?"

"The Graham homestead. Mr Graham is one of your father's customers. I took her there and left her along with my load, but I haven't been back since." The uneasiness he'd felt at leaving the girl in such a remote place returned to him. But Mr Moran had paid well for taking the human cargo along with the timber, nails, rope, canvas and other building materials to Bartholomew Graham's newly acquired land. Christopher couldn't afford to turn down business even though he hadn't liked the idea of taking the girl along the Hawkesbury River and leaving her, but it was none of his business. It wasn't up to Christopher to tell Mr Moran how to behave.

"When will you be returning to that place?" Miss Moran asked.

"I have no idea. If I'm lucky, when your father wants to send more goods to Mr Graham."

The groom cleared his throat and stared up at them with curiosity.

"Well, I must take my leave." Christopher bowed politely.

"Wait!" she said, as he began to descend the steps. "You said you saw something reminiscent of her in my face..."

"Yes," he said, "but I may have been mistaken."

She seemed aware of the similarity, and he was tempted to ask if they were related, but really, it was none of his business. Her mouth opened as if she wanted to say something, but she remained silent.

The horse stamped, showing his impatience to be off and Christopher turned to go. "If I find anything out," he said, "how can I get word to you? Or perhaps you have a message I can take to her?"

Abigail sighed and bit her lower lip. "I don't know. Mama accompanies me everywhere. I'm rarely alone unless I'm sketching in the grounds. Perhaps if my maid is in town, she might find you at the quay?"

Don't give her your address! He warned himself. *Don't, don't, don't!*

But his mouth had already started speaking. "If the Hannah Elizabeth is not in port, it may be hard to find me. But your maid could call at my lodgings. It's not far from the quay –Riley's Lodging House, in Cooper's Alley. It's a turning off Spring Row. My landlady would pass a message on to me."

Her eyes lit up. "Thank you, Mr Randall I would be much obliged if you could find Lottie," she called after him as he hurried down the steps towards the waiting horse and groom.

He was angry with himself for giving her hope. If her father didn't want him to make further deliveries to Bartholomew Graham, Christopher would have no reason to venture along the tributary where he lived, so no means of delivering any messages to the girl, nor of finding any news. Guilt prevented him from looking back at her and not only because he knew she was pinning her hopes on him for news of the girl but because it had gone against his conscience to have left Lottie Jackson there in the first place.

As Abigail made her way up the grand staircase back to her bedroom, she wondered if she'd ever be at ease when she was in the company of a young man. On both occasions when she'd met Mr Randall, her reason had fled, and she'd become embarrassed and tongue-tied. Even with her intended, Hugh, she hadn't known what to say although it had been of no importance because he spoke easily and with confidence, barely requiring her to say anything at all.

Now she was alone, she had a chance to re-run the conversation she'd just had with Mr Randall. So, it hadn't been her imagination, she'd been correct, there was a similarity between her and Lottie, and it seemed he'd noticed it too although he'd been reluctant to say so. Abigail was halfway up the stairs when she stopped still. Anne Ferguson's whispered gossip echoed through her memory. The newly-married Samuel Thornton had three children out of wedlock, and they all bore a striking resemblance to their father – and therefore, a resemblance to each other. Abigail grabbed the banister as she began to sway. That was it! Papa had fathered another child with a woman other than Mama. Presumably, her mother knew Papa had been unfaithful, and that Lottie was his daughter. It was hardly surprising Mama had been in such a heightened state of anxiety when she knew Lottie had been at Westervale Hall. It all made sense. Papa's rush to get rid of Lottie and banish her to some ungodly place along a remote river, as well as his uncharacteristically harsh behaviour during the last few days. And that would explain Mama's sobs and the muffled yet unmistakable sound of angry conversation between her parents that had erupted every so often since Abigail had shown her mother Lottie's sampler with the initials.

Lottie had said her mother and sister had died, so it had all been buried in the past... until now. No wonder neither of her parents wanted to hear a word said about Lottie and it was hardly surprising they were so keen to marry Abigail off to Hugh Hanville who they hoped would take her to England. With Lottie stranded along the Hawkesbury and Abigail in England, her parents could go back to their comfortable life together. Papa's business empire had been built on his impeccable reputation but if an earlier indiscretion were to come to light, who knew what might happen?

So, Abigail had a half-sister? Did Lottie know of their relationship? She hadn't said anything and when Abigail had asked where her father was she'd said she'd never known him. That could be true even if she knew his identity. But surely, she'd have said something? Or would she?

If she'd been as self-serving as Mama claimed all servants were, she would definitely have told Abigail. But if not?

A footman walked into the entrance hall and looked at her quizzically.

"Is something ailing you, miss?" he asked.

Keeping her voice as steady as she could, she replied she was fine and as he walked away, she carried on up the stairs to her bedroom.

CHAPTER SIX

Christopher gripped the tiller of the Hannah Elizabeth as he guided the boat along the snaking river. He swatted yet another mosquito that had landed on his neck. The air was thick and heavy, and he knew there'd be a storm before long. Here, the Hawkesbury was narrower than at any other point they'd passed on this journey. On the larboard side were long stretches of mangroves – their tangled roots visible above the green water. They gave way here and there to narrow strips of sandy beach. Behind them, cliffs rose upwards, fringed on the top with wispy, grey-green trees. To starboard, reeds topped with feathery plumage lined the banks and behind those, the river oaks were alive with colourful birds perched on the gnarled branches.

Christopher knew Bartholomew Graham's land was around the next bend. Already the rain had begun – fat drops were hurled down with such force, they stung his skin. Djalu, his servant grinned at him, his white teeth brilliant against his black skin and his wet, curly hair plastered to his forehead. Djalu knew every twist and turn of this river because his tribe had once roamed the Hawkesbury unhindered before the white man had arrived and gradually laid claim to plots along the shores.

Christopher had learned some of the Eora language and Djalu had picked up sufficient English so that between them, they could communicate and sail the boat with ease. To call Djalu a servant wasn't strictly correct. He came and went as he pleased, occasionally disappearing for a night or two to return to his tribe, but he always returned, and Christopher relied on him to navigate the more remote regions and tributaries such as this, on which Bartholomew Graham had decided to settle.

Overlying the fresh smells of the mud and vegetation that were usually associated with a river, Christopher could detect a strong odour. His pulse quickened as he recognised the sharp tang of woodsmoke – not unusual, as smoke from native fires could often be seen curling upwards towards the sky. But this smell was strong, and even the rain was failing to wash the air clean.

From time to time, natural blazes began with a flash of lightning striking a tree and sometimes the native people carried out controlled burning of the bush but judging by Djalu's reaction, the fire that had caused this smell was something more serious. His heavy brows drew together, and his eyes moved rapidly, scanning both banks as if he believed something was amiss.

As they rounded the corner, Christopher stared in disbelief at what had been the Graham homestead. The foliage at the edge of the clearing on which the house had once stood, was still silver-green – although scorched in places. However, the house and outbuildings had been reduced to twisted, blackened beams rising from a layer of thick, grey ash. Now, all that was left of Graham's farm were a few chickens that scratched amongst the ruins.

Christopher felt sick. This was not the first home that had been attacked and it probably wouldn't be the last. Bartholomew Graham had a reputation for cruelty and intolerance, and he'd chosen to settle in the middle of nowhere, knowing the risks. However, Lottie had not wanted to come, and Christopher had been responsible for bringing her. It hadn't sat well with his conscience, especially when he'd met Graham. Such a powerful man with a hard face and dark, dangerous eyes. He needed men to help him tame the land, not a slight girl like Lottie. Christopher had earned quite a sum for that journey because not only had he been paid for the delivery, but he'd picked up crops from settlers on his return and the entire trip had been very profitable. Nevertheless, Christopher had been unable to banish the image of the girl crying as he'd sailed away.

Djalu took over the tiller as Christopher climbed over the side of the boat and waded through the water towards the sand of Graham's Cove. As he approached, the chickens scuttled into the undergrowth, jerking their heads, and clucking indignantly. Christopher took a deep breath and walked up the beach toward the ash and charred remains. With hands cupped around his mouth, he threw his head back and shouted, "Hello!"

With much flapping of wings and shrill shrieks of alarm, a flock of yellow birds rose out of the river oaks by the clearing. However, other than the eerie echoes of his cry that bounced off the cliffs on the other bank and drifted back across the water, there was no other human sound.

Djalu tied up the boat and joined Christopher on the sand. Slowly, he shook his head. "Girl not here. We go."

This had the appearance of a native attack and Christopher suspected Djalu believed the occupants of the house had been killed. The two men headed back down the beach towards the Hannah Elizabeth and after clambering aboard, they propelled her out into the middle of the river.

There was no point tarrying. Christopher had detoured to find news of Lottie and he now had to hurry if he was going to get to all the homesteads where he'd promised to pick up produce to transport to Sydney Cove.

Christopher's first stop was at the next settlement along the river – the Landers property. He intended to ask if the owner knew what had happened at Graham's Cove although, there was such a great distance between the two homesteads, it was unlikely he'd even know of the attack.

Two dogs bounded to the jetty. They ran back and forth, barking madly and baring their teeth, as the boat approached and seconds later, Joshua Landers appeared and called the dogs to heel.

"Come up to the house," he said to Christopher, ignoring Djalu, "Margaret! We have a visitor!" he yelled over his shoulder.

Once in the house, Landers introduced his wife who welcomed Christopher, and made him a dish of tea.

"Ah! Graham..." Landers paused and shook his head sadly when Christopher told him what they'd found further along the river. "Foolish man. Always thought he knew best. He kidnapped two native lads and tried to make them work for him. Their tribe came to take them home. And then took their revenge."

"So, you knew his house had been attacked?" Christopher asked.

Landers concentrated on filling his pipe, but eventually, he nodded.

"How did you hear?" Christopher asked.

"Oh..." Landers drew on the stem of his pipe and glanced upwards as he inhaled. "Word gets around these parts," he added.

Christopher wondered how word could possibly get around in such a remote and unpopulated region. "There was a girl working with Graham, do you know what happened to her?" he asked.

Landers glanced towards Margaret; his smile now gone. "What's it to you?" His face was guarded.

"A friend asked me to find out how she was faring," Christopher said.

"And the name of your friend?" Margaret butted in sharply.

"Miss Abigail Moran." Christopher detected yet another glance between husband and wife but neither of them spoke.

The curtain that hung in the doorway to another room fluttered and Christopher wondered if one of the dogs had got into the house, but it moved aside to reveal a girl. She gripped the sides of her apron nervously and observed him through enormous eyes.

"Lottie?" Christopher couldn't believe this girl was the one who'd been so distraught when he'd delivered her to Bartholomew Graham. "You're alive?"

Margaret stepped forward and placed a restraining hand on her arm. "You don't have to tell anyone anything, lass." Her eyes flashed a warning towards Lottie, who smiled at her.

"I know Mrs Landers," Lottie said.

"But how did you escape?" Christopher asked. It was hard to imagine how she could have made her way along the riverbank through so many miles of difficult terrain.

"I'm not sure. I was overcome with the smoke and the next thing I remember was waking up here," Lottie said.

"The first Margaret and I knew about it was when several natives arrived in a canoe. They lifted Lottie out, brought her up to the house and left her outside," Landers said, "they never said a word. Just put her down and walked off back to their canoe."

"She's been here ever since and that's the way we like it," said Margaret folding her arms across her chest, "so we don't need anyone interfering." She glared at Christopher.

"Mr and Mrs Landers have been very kind to me," Lottie said, "I'd like to stay here and work for them. I don't want Mr Moran to know where I am, or he'll move me somewhere even more remote. Please, don't tell him!"

"No, of course not. I need only tell Mr Moran that Graham's Landing has been destroyed and that I saw no sign of survivors. That much is true. I suspect he'll be more interested in losing a client than..." He paused, not wanting to add 'than a woman who'd been accused of theft.' That was unnecessarily harsh.

"I'm not a thief," Lottie said firmly, guessing what Christopher had been reluctant to say. "I was wrongly accused. Miss Moran lent me her parasol. I would never have stolen from her. She'd been so kind to me." She paused and then added, "You said she asked after me. Would she have enquired if I'd stolen something from her?"

Christopher nodded, finished his tea, and rose to leave. Miss Moran had also told him she'd lent a parasol to Lottie, so that appeared to be the truth. And anyway, it was none of his business. Thomas Moran had told him Lottie had admitted she'd taken something from his daughter and had agreed to work for Bartholomew Graham rather than be arrested. At the time, he hadn't thought anything of it. Sydney was full of criminals. But now, he was beginning to wonder what was going on. However, whatever the rights and wrongs of this situation, he had to keep on the right side of Mr Moran if his business was to survive. Lottie was safe and happy, so at least his conscience was salved.

As the dogs began barking, Landers hurried away to find out what was disturbing them, and Lottie accompanied Christopher back to his boat.

"Please, Mr Randall, I implore you, don't tell anyone you've found me."

"But Miss Moran specifically asked me to look for you. Surely I can tell her."

"No! It's best she doesn't know."

"You believe she'll tell her father?"

"No, it's not that. It's... it's just better she believes I died."

"It's one thing failing to reveal I know where you are to Mr Moran but you're asking me to look Miss Moran in the eyes and lie."

Lottie touched his arm. "Please, Mr Randall! If you have any kindness in you at all, you'll do as I ask."

Christopher increased his pace. This had nothing to do with him and yet he was completely entangled in the sorry situation.

"Wait, Mr Randall! I'll tell you why she mustn't know but you must promise me on your life not to tell her."

Christopher looked at the Hannah Elizabeth and Djalu, waiting to leave. They had a long journey ahead of them and he was keen to go.

"You have my word."

"Miss Moran is my sister, but she has no idea, and she must never find out."

"Your sister?" There was a resemblance between the two girls. It was certainly possible. Thomas Moran might have fathered children all over Sydney. "But I don't understand why you're so concerned," he said, "I'm sure it would be a shock but after all, she's the legitimate daughter of Thomas Moran. Why are you trying to protect her?"

"The legitimate...? Oh, I see. You believe Mr Moran is our father? No, my mother died giving birth to Miss Moran aboard a convict ship before we'd even arrived in Sydney. I was three years old, and I was told my sister had died. I only discovered recently that she was taken away and given to the Morans."

"How can you be sure of this?" He'd stopped on the jetty, all haste to return to the boat forgotten. This was completely unexpected.

"I recognised a distinctive birthmark on her hand. It's a Dolphin's Kiss. And her birthday coincides with my sister's. But she must never know. Her life would change forever. Do you understand now why this must be kept secret?" She caught hold of his sleeve, her eyes pleading with him to understand.

"I assume that's why Thomas Moran sent you out here?" Everything now made sense.

"He didn't say so, but yes, it seems likely. Please, Mr Randall, swear you'll keep this secret!"

He gave her his word. It would be easy enough to conceal her existence from Thomas Moran but although he told himself it was nothing to him, he was dreading lying to Abigail Moran.

Abigail had endured two of the longest, most tedious weeks of her life, confined to Westervale Hall. Mrs Hippesley had visited but Mama had not left them alone, preventing Abigail from asking about Lottie. Neither had Mr Randall contacted her. Hugh, however had written and her heart had soared until she read his brief letter. He'd been delayed in Parramatta as his business negotiations had taken longer than expected.

Would there be no end to this dreariness?

And then, a letter had arrived from Mama's sister, Patience, giving Abigail an idea. She wondered whether she and Mama could go to stay with her aunt in Parramatta. A chance encounter with Hugh might remind him of his marriage proposal and prompt a speedy return, or even press him to agree to a date. Then, at least she could help Mama plan the wedding and as soon as she and Hugh were married, there might be an opportunity to look for Lottie and perhaps engage her as a servant.

When Abigail suggested visiting Aunt Patience, she could see from Mama's expression that she was torn. Papa was overseeing a large government building project on the far side of Sydney, where he'd remain for several days, and her mother always hated being home alone. However, she loved to visit her sister and the idea they might accidentally meet Hugh was appealing, but it would mean leaving Westervale Hall in the hands of the servants – something Abigail knew disturbed Mama.

It didn't take too much persuasion before Mama agreed to the trip. A message was sent to Aunt Patience and after receiving a reply the next day, the servants were told to pack so they could leave the following morning. However, that evening, Mama complained of a headache and sickness and Abigail felt guilty, suspecting it had been her suggestion that had provoked Mama's attack. Anything that made her mother anxious seemed to upset her, and she'd only just recovered from her indisposition after she'd seen Lottie's sampler. Nevertheless, the disappointment of not going to Parramatta cut into Abigail deeply and her lack of ability to influence any part of her life chafed like a new pair of boots.

"I suppose I must unpack?" Molly asked, her lips pursed in indignation. She'd been going to accompany Abigail and had been looking forward to seeing more of Ben Armitage who was assisting the carriage driver on the trip.

"Packing up! Unpacking!" Molly muttered under her breath, "'Tis a shame you can't go alone," she added with a sly look at Abigail, "You could ask Mistress..."

Excitement rose in Abigail's chest. It was possible Mama would agree to her going ahead. Unlikely, but possible. After all, as soon as Mama felt better, she could join them in Parramatta.

At first, Mama was reluctant, but eventually, when Abigail pointed out Aunt Patience was expecting them, she agreed, and Abigail ran back to her room before Mama had a chance to change her mind. As she stopped Molly unpacking the valise, it occurred to her she might order the driver to make a detour into Sydney so she could visit Mr Randall's lodgings to see if he had news of Lottie. But it seemed too complicated. News of a detour would get back to her parents and how could she explain such a diversion? But suppose Mama thought she was safe with Molly at Aunt Patience's house, while Aunt Patience and Molly thought she was still with Mama...?

It could be done, Abigail was sure.

Mama would believe Abigail had left early, travelling in the carriage with Molly and the luggage. However, Abigail would instruct Molly to tell Aunt Patience she'd delayed a while in Westervale Hall and would come with Mama as soon as she was well, and the carriage had returned for them.

As soon as Molly and the luggage had left, Abigail would saddle a horse and ride to Sydney. Once she'd located Mr Randall's boarding house, she'd find out about Lottie. If she hurried, she could arrive at Parramatta shortly after the carriage or perhaps even catch it up. Of course, Aunt Patience wouldn't be happy she'd ridden alone to Parramatta, but it would be too late to do anything about it. And with any luck, she wouldn't think to mention it to Mama when she finally arrived.

She didn't like the deceit involved but she could see no other way to try to make things up to Lottie. It wasn't her fault that Papa had strayed all those years ago. If Lottie truly was Papa's daughter, then the Moran family had treated her outrageously and Abigail would only be putting things right. And who would be hurt? Mama could rest until she was better, Molly could spend time with Ben, Aunt Patience wouldn't mind when her sister or niece arrived, so long as they stayed a few days... And Abigail could finally get news about Lottie. It was a perfect plan.

Once the carriage had left just before first light, Abigail took the brown servant's cloak and the cap Molly had bought her and put them in her bag. She'd intended to remove the fine green riding habit Molly had dressed her in and to wear all the servant's clothes but now she'd been laced into her stays, it would take too long to change without a maid's assistance and anyway, once she'd finished in Sydney, she could hardly arrive at Aunt Patience's house looking like a pauper. That would raise too many questions. Once in town, she'd put the cloak on to conceal the riding habit and if she arranged it carefully, she could hide the ruffled front of her shirt and the green skirts. Then, she'd replace her smart green hat with the cap. No one would recognise her and so nothing would get back to her parents. As soon as she was on the road to Parramatta, she could remove the cloak and cap.

Side-saddle, she trotted down the drive sedately, her mouth dry and her heart pumping, fearing that at any moment her mother might send someone to call her back. The closer she got to the gates, the more she urged the horse onwards until with a gasp of delight, she turned onto the path and was no longer in sight of Westervale Hall.

It wasn't yet light but the waterfront in Sydney was already busy. It had been a disastrous few days for Christopher. He'd been expecting to return from his last trip to the Hawkesbury laden with produce for the market and had worried his boat might not be large enough to carry all that was required. However, one of the farmer's crops had been attacked by grubs and there was insufficient to send to town. Another had refused to pay the agreed amount, saying he'd give Christopher the rest on his return and a third had been bitten by a snake and had died. Very little profit had been made on that trip.

And now the Moran cargo that Christopher was expecting to carry to Joshua Landers and several of the other settlers, had not arrived at the quayside ready for loading. He'd have to leave with or without Mr Moran's goods within the next half hour as the tide would turn and the weather was closing in. Christopher knew that Mr Moran was supervising some new government storehouses on the far side of Sydney and in his absence, there'd obviously been some confusion about the delivery. Now, Christopher feared he'd be blamed for the missing items.

Like a handful of seawater, his dreams were trickling through his fingers despite all his planning, hard work and risk-taking on the dangerous trip to the Hawkesbury.

The deteriorating weather conditions had evidently persuaded several other captains of small boats against setting sail, and they made their way along the quay to wait for the weather to improve. But Christopher was committed to setting sail whether the conditions were favourable or not. And the heavy black clouds that were gathering on the horizon suggested it would not be favourable on this trip. Djalu eyed the impending storm too, rubbing his knuckles together; impatient to set off. Christopher knew he'd seen the bad weather before the clouds had even begun to gather.

Djalu looked questioningly as if to ask whether the trip would go ahead. With a sigh, Christopher gave a curt nod. The two men had developed a way of communicating which didn't always require words and he knew Djalu had understood they'd be leaving shortly even though the boat would only be half-full. Already the first instalment of the money borrowed for the Hannah Elizabeth was due. Christopher could just cover it with what he'd already earned, but he needed to build up more capital quickly if he was to meet the next payment. He glanced along the wharf again, looking for Moran's cart, hoping the delivery had been slightly delayed rather than neglected or forgotten. He gripped a coil of rope tightly, fighting back the urge to hurl it into the sea in frustration.

"Mr Randall!"

Further along the quay, he saw a girl in a cap and brown cloak walking towards him, holding the reins of a horse. As she moved her arm to wave at him, a flash of green skirt that was too fancy to be that of a servant could be seen beneath her cloak and a blonde curl escaped from beneath the cap.

Miss Moran? It couldn't be.

But the closer she drew, the more certain he was. What was she doing there? For a second, he wondered if she'd have news of her father's delivery, but then dismissed the thought. Mr Moran would hardly send his daughter to a place like this at such an early hour. Already, two drunken men who were staggering arm in arm, had stopped to try to buy her services and had only retreated when she'd raised her riding crop.

"Mr Randall?" Her voice was now full of alarm.

He clambered out of the boat. "Miss Moran! What are you doing here? Are you lost?"

"I... I came to your lodgings to ask if you have any news of Lottie. I was told you weren't home but that you'd most likely be here, so I came directly to find you. I... I had no idea it would be so... so..." Her voice trailed off and he could only imagine the suggestions that had been made to her as she'd found her way to the far end of the quay where the Hannah Elizabeth was berthed.

"This isn't a safe place for you," he said, more sharply than he'd intended. In suddenly appearing, she'd made things even more complicated for him. He could hardly set sail and leave her alone and defenceless on the quay.

Christopher took her arm and turned her around, ready to lead her to a safer place. If he hurried, he could still make the voyage. Djalu joined them on the quayside, and Christopher signalled to him to be ready to cast off on his return.

With remarkable spirit, she pulled her arm away from him. "I've come to find out about Lottie. Have you made any enquiries? Have you discovered anything?"

A low rumble on the horizon reminded Christopher of the impending storm.

"I beg your pardon, Miss Moran, I'm afraid we must leave immediately. But rest assured, I'll find you on my return. Now I must return you to the rest of your party..." He tried to take her arm again, but she pulled it away.

"There is no party for me to return to. I am here alone."

"But why?" She obviously had no idea of the dangers to a young, unaccompanied woman in this part of town. Was he going to have to escort her back to Westervale Hall? He almost groaned in frustration.

"I've already told you, Mr Randall," she said with disarming candour, "I want to know if you've discovered anything about Lottie?"

Christopher and Djalu exchanged glances. "I... We... that is..." He glanced back at the boat unable to look her in the eye.

"Please tell me if you know something, Mr Randall."

She was begging and as he made the mistake of looking at her stricken face, his resolve crumbled. She clearly wasn't going to leave until he told her something, despite her anxiety at being amongst so many pressing bodies and coarse comments.

How much could he tell her, yet still keep his promise to Lottie?

"We went to Graham's Cove to look for her but..." He hesitated.

Should he simply say that no one had been there?

Before he could decide how to proceed, Djalu jumped in, "House all burned. No one there. Girl gone." He signalled with his eyes that they should leave. "Now we go?" he said to Christopher.

Christopher looked at him in horror, but it was too late.

"The house was burned? You mean there was a fire? What happened? Where is Lottie? Was she hurt? Was she...?" Colour drained from her face.

Christopher had the overwhelming urge to enfold her in his arms. Her face was as grey as the ashes that were all that remained of Graham's house and now, although her mouth was open, no sound came out as she took the news in.

"I'm afraid I don't know, Miss Moran," Christopher said. His spirits sank. Now he couldn't simply take her somewhere safe, and leave. She'd need someone to comfort her. If only Djalu had left it to him to explain, although he suspected that whatever he'd said may not have satisfied her.

"Are you leaving for the Hawkesbury now?" she asked.

He nodded.

"Then you must take me with you, and I can look for her."

Well, she had spirit. Nevertheless, she had no idea what she was asking.

"The Hawkesbury is no place for a woman—" he began.

"Then what business did you have taking Lottie?" she asked.

He and Djalu exchanged glances again. How could he say that her father had paid him well and he'd taken the money and turned away, not wishing to see?

"I won't get in your way, Mr Randall. I simply want to look for her myself."

"No, Miss Moran. I'm afraid that won't be possible under any circumstances."

"If you're worried about payment, I'll be able to pay you on our return I have much jewellery that I can sell."

"That won't be necessary, but please believe me when I tell you I simply cannot take you to the Hawkesbury."

"Cannot or will not?" Her jaw was now clenched as were her fists.

"Please, Miss Moran, I must set sail now. I'll find a way to speak to you on my return. I give you my word." He placed his hand on his heart. Perhaps he could ask Lottie to release him from the promise when he told her how determined her sister had been to see her. Surely, she'd understand. But already the dawn light was dimming as the black clouds rolled in and men had started to leave the quay until the weather had done its worst.

"No! I can see you both know more than you're telling me, and I want to know what it is. You have no idea how hard it was for me to arrange to come here today without my parents knowing and it's unlikely I'll be able to return."

"Randall! Randall!" The driver of a loaded cart urged his horse towards the Hannah Elizabeth. "Good heavens, man, I was afeared you might have left! A carriage overturned on the road here and it took me an' Robbie ages to get through. I'd have laid money on you being gone, what with that squall comin' in," the driver said, leaping down onto the quayside.

It was the Moran cart, loaded high, and Christopher wondered how long it would take to transfer everything onto the boat and whether there would still be time. If Moran's two men helped, he estimated that he and Djalu could just do it. But first, there was the matter of the girl.

"Please, Miss Moran, go home. I'll ask your father's driver to escort you back to Westervale Hall and I promise I'll get a message to you on my return."

To his relief, she nodded and handed the reins of the horse to the driver, who tied them to the cart.

At last, things were going Christopher's way. The storm seemed to have veered slightly and although it would be rough when they made it out to sea, at least the journey to the Port Jackson heads wouldn't be as bad as he'd anticipated. With four men loading the cargo, they'd soon have it aboard and Miss Moran would be safely escorted home.

The men worked tirelessly, heedless of the weight of the timber, tools and bags of nails until they'd finished. Once Djalu and Robbie had picked up the nails that had spilt out of one of the bags in the cart during the journey, and Christopher had checked the list the driver held out for him, they were finished, and they ran to the boat. They set sail as the first heavy drops of rain began to fall.

Jane Moran opened one eye and glared at the maid who'd dared to waken her.

"Beggin' your pardon, Mistress, but Mrs Hippesley is here wishing to talk to you." The maid bobbed a curtsey at the end of Jane's bed, repeatedly smoothing her apron.

"I don't care who it is! I told you I didn't want to be disturbed!" Jane placed her hand over her eyes to keep out the mid-morning sun that was bursting into the room despite the heavy curtains. "I am indisposed! Please tell her to go away. I shall contact her when I am better. And do not dare to disturb me again!"

"B...But, Mistress..." The maid was almost sobbing. "She said 'tis a matter of great urgency and she won't leave until she speaks with you."

Jane sighed. Perhaps there'd been a fire in the emporium and her gowns had been destroyed. That would be most serious... "Very well! Fetch my dressing gown."

"Yes, Mistress," the maid said, holding the gown up for Jane to slip on, then rushing to fetch slippers.

Jane tucked her hair inside a turban. "What are you waiting for, girl?"

"Beggin' your pardon, Mistress but there are two of them."

"Two of them...? Two of what? Slippers?"

But the maid had fled, and it wasn't until Jane saw the two figures waiting on the Turkey rug in the withdrawing room that she realised what the foolish girl had meant.

"What are you doing here?" she asked the smaller, rounder woman who was standing next to Mrs Hippesley. It was Mrs Riley who'd once worked in Westervale Hall as a wet nurse. "I demand to know what's going on!"

"And that," said Mrs Hippesley sharply, "is exactly why we've come. I suggest you sit down, Mrs Moran."

"We've come to talk about Miss Abigail and her... er... beginnings," Mrs Riley said.

"Beginnings?" Jane glared at the two women.

"Beginnings. On the Lady Amelia—"

Jane held up her hand, cutting Mrs Riley off. "And exactly how much money are you demanding to keep this information quiet?"

Mrs Riley took a deep breath, puffed out her already immense bosom and took a step towards Mrs Moran. "How dare you! We don't want your money! I suckled that child meself! I've never told no one about her beginnings. Not that there was any shame in being born to Mary Jackson because she was a fine woman and worth ten o' you!" Mrs Riley's lip curled in contempt as she looked Jane up and down. "We're not asking for a penny. We'll keep this quiet for the girl and her ma's sake and so will all the other women who were there when Mary died."

"All the other...?" Jane's heart nearly stopped. How many people knew?

"Well, of course! There were a large group of us who tried to save Mary. It weren't hard for us to work out why we were told a healthy baby had died and yet one of the governor's men who happened to be an acquaintance of your husband was seen carrying a wailing, swaddled bundle off the ship. But we've all kept that secret for years out of respect to Mary Jackson and her daughters and it'll probably go to our graves with us."

"And, your point is?" Jane's gaze flickered back and forth between the two women.

"My point is, Mrs Moran, that Miss Abigail knows too. She came knocking at my door asking if one of my lodgers had left word about a girl. Of course, I recognised 'er and we 'ad a nice little chat. It didn't take me long to work out what was what. I followed her, but I'm a bit slow these days, an' I lost 'er on the quay. I saw your husband's delivery man and he'd lost sight of 'er too. But I reckon I know where she's gone."

"Gone? She's gone to Parramatta to stay with my sister," Jane said, her voice faint with doubt.

Mrs Riley shook her head. "More like the Hawkesbury."

Jane clutched her throat and moaned.

"Well, there ain't much you can do about that till the Hannah Elizabeth gets back but hark my words, you have a bigger problem now and if you care about your family, you'll take heed."

When Mrs Riley had finished, Jane's face was white with shock. "These are wicked lies! How would you know details such as those?"

Mrs Riley laughed. "I live in the middle of Sydney. I know everyone. There ain't much that gets past me."

Mrs Riley jabbed her finger at her former employer's wife. "You might look down on the likes o' people what have worn the broad arrow and served their time, but let me tell you, we look after our own. Pity you can't say the same for people o' your class..."

She nodded at Mrs Hippesley and together, without being dismissed, the two women left.

Jane's head was throbbing as if her skull would burst. For years, she'd been tormented by fears that the secret would be exposed, laying her family open to ridicule. Thomas had repeatedly assured her he would act swiftly to silence anyone who threatened them, much as he'd done by sending their cook to Norfolk Island, but now, if Mrs Riley was to be believed, many people knew the secret... and had known for years. And even more unbelievably, they'd kept quiet to honour Mary Jackson's memory and to protect Abigail and Lottie. Jane had spent years consumed by doubt and dread and now, it seemed it had all been for naught – there had been no danger at all. Jane stopped herself giving in to the hysterical laughter that bubbled up inside. There was too much to do.

She had to write to Thomas telling him to return immediately. They must wait for Abigail to return. But now, there was something most pressing – and shocking – to attend to. It concerned Hugh Hanville.

CHAPTER SEVEN

Abigail felt sick and not only because of the motion of the rolling boat. The fury and self-righteous indignation that had driven her to creep aboard the Hannah Elizabeth and hide while Mr Randall and the native servant had been distracted, had drained away to be replaced by the numbing realisation that she'd behaved in an utterly reckless manner. She tried to rekindle the anger she'd felt earlier in an attempt to justify her foolishness.

First, she'd never been anywhere as disconcerting as the wharf – it was nothing like the Sydney she knew, where women could stroll safely without crowds of uncouth oafs milling about and jostling them. Her horse, and especially her whip, had given her the confidence to ignore most of the coarse comments and to push her way through.

Then, when she'd found Mr Randall, he and his native servant had obviously known something about Lottie that they'd been reluctant to share with her and if it hadn't been for the servant blurting out about a fire, she was certain Mr Randall wouldn't have mentioned it. A fire! There'd been a fire and he hadn't bothered to find out where Lottie was. And if all that hadn't been enough, he'd refused to take her to the Hawkesbury to find out. She'd said she wouldn't be any trouble; she'd just sit quietly and make a few enquiries amongst the neighbours when she got there – something Mr Randall could easily have done on discovering the fire.

The arrival of her father's men had also forced her hand. She'd tried to conceal herself behind the horse so they didn't see her because they'd be sure to tell Papa, but before she could stop him, Mr Randall had asked the men to escort her home. The indignity of being taken to Westervale Hall by two of Papa's men! Of course, Mr Randall would have no idea what a risk she'd taken in coming to Sydney on her own. If her parents found out, they'd be furious and... And what? What would they do? She had no idea. Lock her in her room? But Hugh would be back soon, and they'd have to let her out. Hugh. What would he think about her rashness?

This could all have gone so perfectly, with no one knowing where she was if only Mr Randall had done as she'd asked. She could have been on her way to Parramatta now – indeed, she might even have been there taking tea with Aunt Patience.

However, reviving her anger was neither soothing her guilt nor her fears and although she could understand and justify her earlier feelings, she couldn't defend her actions in hiding away.

The barrel, behind which she'd squeezed herself, shifted slightly as the boat rose, then crashed into the waves and she was now even more squashed against a crate. The seas were much rougher than she'd expected. She braced herself. Might she be crushed? It was already hard to breathe. Enough was enough! She would appear completely foolish, but she must show herself and beg Mr Randall's forgiveness and ask him not to tell Papa. Once he'd returned to Sydney, she'd see if she could retrieve her horse from her father's men and depending on the time, either ride back to Westervale Hall or carry on to Aunt Patience. And if she asked, perhaps the men wouldn't tell Papa. Yes, that might save the situation. However, first, she must endure the displeasure of Mr Randall...

But how? The sea was now so wild, the only reason she wasn't being tossed about in the boat was that she was crammed in so tightly, she could barely move. She'd been crouching for so long, her feet had lost feeling and her legs were numb. Rain drummed on the tarpaulin that was tied over the barrel and crate between which she was hiding, and she noted with alarm that water was slopping back and forth over the toes of her boots. That was surely too much water to be safe in a boat? Were they sinking?

She strained to hear anything above the howling wind and the flapping and slapping of sails, tarpaulins and ropes, but all sounds from the busy quay had been drowned out by the roaring of the storm and for a second, she wondered if the boat had slipped its moorings and was being tossed about in the bay prior to being sunk. She'd heard Mr Randall and the native come aboard earlier, shouting to each other, but the wind whipped away their words. Bare, black feet had scurried back and forth in front of her, bracing themselves as if the native who owned them was pulling on something heavy. But for some time, there had been no voices, just the raging wind, the roar of thunder, the crackle of lightning and the smash of the waves against the hull. Had the sea washed the men overboard?

The bow of the Hannah Elizabeth was thrown up into the air and just as Abigail feared the heavy barrel might break free of its restraining ropes and crush her, the boat plunged over the other side of the wave with a sickening lurch. A bone-jarring thud followed as it crashed down into the sea. Water sloshed over her, despite the tarpaulin and she saw with alarm, it was now almost up to her ankles. She must escape from her hiding place beneath the tarpaulin before something fell on her or the boat filled with water and sank. But getting out of her hiding place was easier said than done.

Turning sideways, Abigail managed to slide one shoulder out of the gap as the boat bucked again. The force threw her headlong across the deck in a tangle of cloak and petticoats and she slid through the water that sloshed back and forth, rolling with each pitch and toss of the boat. A wave crashed over the gunwale. It hit her like a slap, drenching her and stinging her eyes as she grabbed blindly for something to hang on to. Through bleary eyes, she'd been relieved to see the figures of the two men still in the boat. Mr Randall bending over the tiller. The native tying up a sail. Well, at least, she wasn't alone. Her cap was snatched from her head by the wind. It was whipped away. If she couldn't find something to hold on to, she'd surely follow it into the churning, spuming waves. She scrabbled desperately to hold on. Everything she touched slipped out of her gloved grasp.

Was that a man's shout? It was impossible to tell with nature roaring around her. She rubbed her arm across her eyes to clear them of the water. The timbers of the hull shuddered at the force of the next mountainous wave that slammed into the boat, covering her in freezing spray. It pricked her skin like needles, stinging her eyes with salt once again. She gasped with shock, choking as the seawater raked at her throat. The boat tilted. She slid into the bulwark and grabbing for a handhold, her fingers closed on nothing. This was the end. She'd be thrown overboard.

A strong hand gripped her wrist and hauled her across the deck. Mr Randall had got her. But as she looked up through salty, rain-soaked eyelids, she realised he was still at the tiller. The native had her in a firm grasp and was pulling off her glove. What was he doing? If she'd had more strength, she'd have resisted but when he placed her hand on a rope, she realised she could steady herself without slipping. She clutched it while he pulled off the other glove. Somehow, he'd managed to brace himself and propel her towards the bulwark beneath the tarpaulin where there were more ropes to hold on to.

She clung on wondering how much longer this dreadful journey would last. They seemed to have been tossed this way and that for hours – perhaps days. Her head throbbed. She was freezing, drenched, sick and bruised. How could such a simple act of kindness as lending someone a parasol have resulted in this?

By the time Christopher had guided the Hannah Elizabeth into the relative shelter of Broken Bay, the steely grey clouds were beginning to roll away revealing glimpses of blue sky. The freezing winds that had been blowing from the Antarctic had subsided to a bracing breeze although his hands were still so cold, it felt as though they were frozen in place, gripping the tiller. However, once they sailed into the Hawkesbury River, he knew the temperature and humidity would begin to rise and he'd thaw out.

The girl was propped against the bulwark, the tarpaulin draped over her, and he couldn't stop himself shaking his head in disbelief at her irresponsible stupidity. Or perhaps it was disbelief in his. He'd actually considered trying to battle the waves to take her back to Sydney once he'd realised that she'd hidden aboard. It had been impossible, of course, and he'd had no alternative but to carry on. Indeed, it was a miracle the Hannah Elizabeth had survived. She was a sturdy boat but the conditions they'd just experienced had been the worst he'd ever endured. And rather than thinking of the safety of Djalu, himself and the boat, he'd considered the needs of the girl.

Fool! She'd caused him untold trouble, but his heart had nearly stopped when she'd been thrown about on the deck unable to hold on. He'd feared that by the time he'd managed to lash down the tiller, she'd have been hurled overboard but thankfully, Djalu had got to her first. And that, of course, had put Djalu at risk too.

Christopher flexed first one hand, then the other, and life slowly returned to his fingers His anger at himself mounted as he relived the journey in the open sea, and he gripped the tiller until his knuckles turned white. From the other end of the boat, Djalu raised his eyebrows questioningly and then glanced at the girl. He'd recognised that Christopher had tried to turn the boat, forcing it into the storm, and he'd cried out a warning in his native tongue – or perhaps it had been a curse – but the howl of indignation had cut through the roaring wind and been sufficient to bring Christopher back to his senses. Attempting to return to Sydney would have been madness.

The girl was asleep. She'd exhausted herself holding on to prevent herself from being thrown out of the boat. Damp curls stuck to her forehead and on one cheek, a bruise stood out, purple against the greenish tinge of her skin. Christopher dragged his eyes away from her. The entrance to the Hawkesbury River still had to be negotiated and this was no time to lose concentration. With the strong winds, they'd made excellent time but there was still a fair way to go before they reached

Joshua Landers' homestead. Before that, however, he'd have to decide which of the sisters to betray.

Abigail could see land to the right and to the left, and the water was calm. Presumably, this was the Hawkesbury River. She hugged her knees to her chest, trying to take up as little space as possible on the cramped deck to keep out of the men's way. They'd been remarkably good-tempered about her being there although she knew she didn't deserve it.

Of all the stupid, thoughtless and impulsive things she'd done, this had exceeded everything by far. If only she could take back the instant when she'd decided to board the boat, but everything had happened so quickly after that, she hadn't had time to think.

Oh, yes you did! A tiny voice told her. *You had plenty of time to think but as usual, you thought you knew best.*

It was true. If only her head would stop spinning and her stomach churning, it might allow her time to consider how she was going to put everything right. At least her hair and clothes were beginning to dry, and she was warming up.

By the time Djalu offered her a drink of water and some dry bread, her stomach had settled enough for her to accept it gratefully. Mr Randall had said that under such circumstances, formalities seemed senseless, and he'd suggested she call him Christopher. She'd happily agreed to him calling her Abigail. He was being much friendlier than she deserved. She'd apologised but he'd merely shaken his head to dismiss her words and the two men had once again exchanged glances as if they were both aware of things about which she knew nothing. Their knowing looks were disconcerting, but she was in no position to criticise. In her current predicament, she had no rights at all. She'd foolishly imposed herself upon them.

After that, she'd kept quiet, not wanting to disturb them at their work. Although they'd delivered a few items to huts and small houses along the banks, most of the cargo was still on board and she yearned to ask how much longer it would be before they reached a town or village. She had so many questions: how long before they got back to Sydney? What happened if they got lost? Were they in any danger?

The banks glided past, and she marvelled at the silence. No, not silence, because the air was filled with the gurgle of water, the whistle of wind through the eucalypts, the calls of birds, the hum of insects and the infrequent cry of an unseen animal. But other than the occasional hushed comment of either Djalu or Christopher, there were no human sounds. She tried to recall all that Papa had said about this region but other than that he was keen to do business with the settlers here, she could remember little of use.

In the steamy heat, the flies swarmed around the boat. Would this journey ever be over? She must have dozed off as she became aware of Christopher kneeling next to her, having handed the tiller to Djalu.

"Miss M... I mean, Abigail. I must ask you to do something for me."

"Yes?" If it made amends, she'd do whatever he asked.

"We're about to make our final stop but I need you to remain out of sight. While Djalu and I unload, I would ask you to remain hidden." He held up the tarpaulin for her to crawl under.

"But I wanted to ask some of the townspeople whether they've seen Lottie."

"Abigail," he said slowly as if speaking to a child, "there *is* no town here. Just the few homesteads you've seen, many spread miles apart like the one where we'll make our last delivery. I shall enquire about Lottie again, but I want you to trust me and to let me ask in my own way. Can you do that for me?"

She bridled at his tone. He was speaking to her as if she might have trouble understanding; nevertheless, she nodded. This was his world and one about which she knew nothing. So, there was no town and therefore no townspeople who might know what had happened. She'd taken such a risk to find out about Lottie to no avail.

The air beneath the tarpaulin was hot and thick with the smell of tar and stagnant water. A mosquito whined by Abigail's ear, and she tried to bat it away, but the hum transferred to her other ear. Something bit her ankle. She brushed her leg and a tiny creature scuttled away. This was intolerable. On Christopher's request, she'd hidden under the tarpaulin before the boat had glided around the bend, so she had no idea where they'd moored nor what manner of place it was.

Voices drifted through the air and Abigail listened intently, wondering how much longer it would be before Christopher came back and told her what he'd discovered. There were no other sounds of human habitation, no wheels trundling along roads, no children playing nor women calling out to each other. Just a few chickens squawking and dogs barking. Then, her breath caught in her throat. Was that Lottie's voice? She strained to hear. It wasn't a voice she was familiar with, only having heard it a few times but the harder she listened, the more certain she was that Lottie was speaking. Or was she?

If Christopher was talking to Lottie, he wouldn't leave her beneath a tarpaulin. Would he? He'd asked her to trust him, and she'd said she would. But he'd kept the fact there'd been a fire from her. Perhaps he couldn't be trusted.

Before she'd had a chance to think, she'd crept out from beneath the tarpaulin. It would have been sensible to have crouched and hidden behind the cargo, but the sudden onslaught of sunlight had dazzled her after the relative darkness beneath the tarpaulin and she stood for a few seconds, shielding her eyes and trying to get her balance. However, it was long enough for the four people who were standing together in a clearing set back from the water's edge to stop speaking and to stare at her.

Abigail gasped.

Christopher was standing with a man and two women, one of whom was Lottie. Until Abigail had appeared, he seemed to have been explaining something, but now, his expression froze and as the others spotted her, Lottie squealed, her hands flying to her face. The older woman put an arm around her shoulders and tried to calm her.

Abigail had not been aware that Djalu was behind her in the boat and now he muttered, "Trouble. Plenty trouble." He shook his head and surveyed her with disbelief.

Christopher strode towards her, a look of exasperation on his face. He swept both hands through his fringe and for a second, paused with palms holding his head. "Why did you not wait as I asked?"

"I...I," stammered Abigail, realising that once again she'd acted without thinking, "You promised me you'd give me news and you didn't..." she began. He'd lied to her but now he was making it sound as if she was at fault. She might have behaved impetuously, but at least she hadn't tried to deceive anyone.

"Well, there's no avoiding it now. For good or ill, now is the time for truth." He stood on the jetty, hands on hips looking down at her in the boat. "Yes, I found the burned-out homestead at Graham's Cove as I said, and I also found Lottie here on my last trip, but she made me promise not to tell you where she was. So, how could I have told you without betraying her trust? I wanted to tell you, but I had promised her first."

If he had slapped her, Abigail couldn't have been more hurt.

"Why doesn't she want me to know she's here?" she whispered.

Christopher leaned forward, offering her his hand, to pull her out of the boat. "I suggest you ask her yourself."

Abigail allowed herself to be hauled onto the jetty. Her self-assurance ebbed with each step as she walked towards the three people who eyed her with disapproval.

"I beg your pardon for causing offence, Lottie but I only wanted to know you were well," she said as she approached.

"To salve your conscience, I reckon," the woman said coldly. You should've kept your distance. If your father takes Lottie away..."

"Oh, but he won't! I won't let him! I won't tell him! I wouldn't do anything to hurt Lottie."

"Are you telling me your father doesn't know you're here?" The woman's voice was mocking.

"No, he doesn't know. He's working away from home—"

"A girl from a family such as yours doesn't just disappear for a day or two without someone asking questions. If your father doesn't know where you are now, he'll find out. And he'll want to know what drove you to the wilds of the Hawkesbury. He'll work it out..."

The woman turned to Lottie who stood awkwardly, her hands bunching the fabric of her apron. "Joshua and I will look out for you, lass." Then turning to Abigail, she said, "I suppose it's you we need to feel sorry for now. Well, best come into the house. What has to be said is best done over a dish of tea. The men can unload while we talk."

Mrs Landers and Lottie busied themselves boiling water and making tea, while Abigail kept out of their way, aware of the strained atmosphere. What on earth had the woman meant when she said they needed to feel sorry for her? Lottie treated Abigail with deference, although Mrs Landers had less reserve and periodically peered at the visitor with hostility.

In an attempt to establish a friendlier atmosphere, Abigail said, "If I've caused you any harm, Lottie, I am truly sorry. That was not my intention." She would be candid, and she would tell Lottie the truth and perhaps that would ease the disquiet. "When I met you and you recognised my birthmark, I suddenly became aware of something in you that was in myself. I know we don't look the same but the first time I saw you, it was as if I was looking into a mirror that partially reflected me. And that set me wondering because for years I've felt as though something was missing from my life."

Lottie gasped and clapped her hand to her mouth.

"And now I realise we're sisters and I wanted to find you and try to put everything right. I can only apologise for our father's actions and tell you that he's never behaved in such an inexplicably severe way before. I believe he's trying to protect my mother but his behaviour towards you was completely unacceptable. It's hardly your fault that he..." She paused, looking for the words that adequately described what he'd done, and yet didn't condemn him.

However, to her surprise, Lottie shook her head and held up a hand to stop her. "I think you may be mistaken."

Mistaken? Had Abigail been wrong? What if the girl wasn't related to her at all? Had her desire to fill what she perceived to be an empty place in her life overwritten her common sense?

"Yes, it's true we're sisters, but not in the way you imagine." Lottie glanced at Mrs Landers who gave a slight shrug as if it didn't matter now if she carried on. Taking a deep breath, Lottie continued, "This is what I wanted to protect you from. We are sisters but not in the way you've assumed. Thomas Moran is neither your father nor mine. The truth is we have different fathers and neither of us is likely to ever know them."

"But how can that be?" Abigail stared at her in disbelief. Papa, not her father? That was inconceivable.

"Our mother died on board a ship shortly after giving birth to you..."

Our mother? Abigail remembered the story Lottie had told her and the sampler she'd made showing the dolphin and the ship. Her mouth was dry. Words died in her throat. She stared at the two women, trying to take in the enormity of Lottie's words.

Papa, not her papa? She, the daughter of a convict? A life lived with two people who weren't her parents? No, it was nonsense. And yet, the likeness between her and Lottie... Papa's harshness. Mama's distress. No, it simply couldn't be true! It was monstrous! Lies! But whose lies?

Who was she?

Lottie crouched next to Abigail, taking her hands. "This was the pain I wanted to spare you." Tears trickled down her cheeks.

"Has nothing in my life been true?" Abigail finally whispered.

"Yes!" Lottie said firmly, "You grew up in a family with parents who loved you and wanted you. Your father acted to protect you."

But the thoughts in Abigail's brain were running in all directions like a pat of butter on a plate that's been left in the sun. The more she tried to hold on to one idea and to consider it, the more it slithered out of reach. She'd once believed there was a space in her life that needed filling, but now, she recognised there was an unbridgeable chasm.

"Unless the lass plans to stay with us, she must leave now, Margaret," Landers called from outside the house. For a second Abigail wondered whether remaining with them might be a good option, but she saw from Mrs Landers' face that it most definitely would not.

Margaret snorted. "Let her stay here and bring down the wrath of Mr Moran on all of us? I don't think so! Well, lass, I'm afraid you must leave. My heart goes out to you, truly it does. This weren't a problem of your making but..."

But what? Abigail wondered, the thoughts in her head spinning as she followed Christopher back to the boat. Lottie had convinced Abigail that her parents had chosen her as their daughter. Over the years, they'd proved their love by always doing their best for her and protecting her from the knowledge of her roots. They'd sent Lottie away so their closely guarded secret would be kept from her and from everyone else. And they'd done all that to protect her and the family name. But now what would happen?

Did they have to know? Suppose she didn't tell them what she'd discovered?

But she hadn't expected to be away so long and as soon as they found out she hadn't been at Westervale Hall, nor at Aunt Patience's house, they'd demand to know where she had been and ultimately, she'd have to tell them. They would guess all the other details. Then what would happen?

Abigail caught up with Christopher and as they stepped onto the wooden jetty, it groaned under their weight. He didn't flinch, appearing not to notice, but the creak served to remind her that however sturdy things seemed, nothing was certain. Even the ground beneath her feet about which she'd once given no thought at all, now threatened to collapse beneath her.

On the return journey, Abigail sat silently, trying to unravel her thoughts. She rehearsed conversations she might have with her parents when she got back, but without knowing her parents' opinions, it was impossible to predict what they might say. So, how could she plan an argument? Nevertheless, questions, explanations, accusations and begging appeals surged through her mind like the waters that raced past the Hannah Elizabeth, carrying them towards Broken Bay and home.

It wasn't until Christopher and Djalu jumped out of the boat and made it fast to the trunk of a tree which was leaning precariously over the river, that she looked up. What were they doing? At first, she thought they'd stopped along the bank but then realised they'd tied up to a tree on a small island in the middle of the river. The sun was so low, the men's shadows stretched from one end of the beach to the other. They couldn't be stopping here, surely, there was no sign of habitation.

She continued to watch the water eddying around the boat hull while she waited for the men to board and set off once again.

"Abigail?" Christopher cleared his throat, clearly embarrassed at disturbing her. "Please allow me to help you ashore. We shall rest here for the night."

She looked up at him in horror. The night? She'd be out here for the whole night? Time had failed to have any meaning as if she'd stepped outside of it but now, if she'd harboured any thoughts that she'd still be able to get home without anyone noticing her absence, they were gone. And for the first time, she allowed Hugh into the muddled mix of questions and thoughts that tumbled around her brain. How would he feel when he discovered she'd spent a night alone with two men? She knew it was childish, but she was tempted to close her eyes and pretend none of this was happening.

"Just for a few hours," he said, "we leave again before first light."

Well, of course, the men would need a break. Abigail was so tired she felt giddy, and she'd done nothing physical at all. So, how much more must they need to rest? She held out her left hand to take his and then pulled it back sharply, extending her right hand instead. Even in the dull, green light that bathed the river, the blemish stood out starkly against the white of her skin. How she loathed it! Now, for the first time, she understood her mother's horror at what must always have reminded her of Abigail's beginnings. It hadn't simply been that her daughter was disfigured, it had been a constant reminder that Abigail wasn't hers. How much pain had the mark caused? After Lottie had recognised it and called it a Dolphin's Kiss, Abigail had begun to accept it but now, it had resulted in so much anguish, she knew she'd detest it forever.

"It may be best to give me both hands," Christopher said, "just to be safe."

Reluctantly, she took both of his hands and as he grasped her tightly, he looked into her eyes and held her gaze. After she was safely on shore, he released her right hand, holding on to her left hand for several seconds longer. Was he trying to tell her the birthmark didn't bother him? No, that wasn't possible. It was simply her tired brain reading something into nothing.

A little later, Djalu stepped out of the thicket that edged the beach and removed several dead animals that dangled from his belt.

"Best not to ask what Djalu's caught," Christopher said with a wink, "but once it's cooked, it will be welcome."

Djalu built a fire and while he placed what Abigail thought looked like

95

large lizards on skewers over the flames, Christopher brought a tarpaulin from the boat and laid it on the sand. Despite the unappealing look of the animals that were cooking, Abigail's mouth watered at the aroma that drifted on the stiffening breeze. She helped collect dried twigs from beneath the trees, holding them in her salt-stiffened skirts. When she returned to the fire, Christopher was cutting lumps from the meat and placing them on large leaves set on the tarpaulin. He handed her one and indicated she should sit.

Abigail sat down and noticed items of clothing strewn on the sand as if someone had undressed as they walked down to the river. Her gaze followed the trail of clothes, and in the water, she saw Djalu duck under the surface, then leap upwards, with water streaming off his naked back. He raised his arms and as water droplets cascaded like diamonds into the river, she saw bands of raised scars and white dotted lines decorating his shoulders and arms. With a cry, he threw his head back and sprang into the air, back arching as he dived into the river and disappeared.

"Where's he gone?" Abigail was aghast at the sudden glimpse of a naked man. It was something so unexpected – frightening yet exhilarating.

"A tribal gathering. Most likely an initiation ceremony. He'll spend the night with his people," Christopher said, sitting down on the tarpaulin.

"Those markings..." she said, "I've never seen anything like them."

"They're spectacular, aren't they? Men and women of the various tribes have different patterns of scars. They're a matter of great pride." He looked down at her left hand that was palm upwards in her lap, hiding the birthmark. She shifted uncomfortably under his scrutiny.

"I wish..." She couldn't finish. This man was a stranger, and she was too ashamed to say that she wished she could accept her blemish. She would give anything to be able to tolerate it, let alone be proud of it.

"Those scars mark the passage into adulthood. No one without them can trade, marry or take part in the ceremonial songs." Christopher paused, then added, "I have a tattoo on my forearm. Not quite the same thing, but similar." He rolled his sleeve up and held his arm near the fire for her to see the anchor inscribed in his skin. "And not quite the same as having a Dolphin's Kiss..."

Abigail squirmed with embarrassment that he'd mentioned it, but she felt bolder in the darkness and after a few seconds, she asked softly, "Do you truly believe that's what it is? A Dolphin's Kiss?"

"Perhaps. I chose an anchor because it represents hope and safety.

Those are the things I wanted to believe the tattoo would bring me. Perhaps what's important about Djalu's scars, my anchor and your Dolphin isn't what they look like. What matters is that we each believe they can deliver dreams."

Deliver dreams. Abigail wasn't sure she had any dreams to deliver. She'd never had anything to strive for and other than the hope she'd marry Hugh Hanville so she could escape her mother's constant disapproval, she had no dreams at all.

"Tell me about your dreams," she said, aware that Mama might not consider that a suitable topic of conversation in polite society. But what did it matter? She was about to spend the entire night with this man in a topsy-turvy, upside-down world in which she now found herself. Years before, Papa had played Blind Man's Buff with her, tying a cloth around her eyes, and spinning her until she had no idea which way she was facing. He would always allow her to find him easily, making noises so she could locate him. Now, she felt as though she'd been spun around and having removed the blindfold, she'd discovered she was in a different world.

Nothing could get her home without anyone missing her. And nothing would change the conversation she must have with her parents to tell them what she'd discovered on her arrival home. But what she did in the meantime, was up to her. She could hardly make the situation worse.

Before Christopher could reply, a cry rang out in the distance, followed by a roar that made the hairs on the back of Abigail's neck prickle. Her hand flew to her mouth. "What was that?"

"I imagine that's Djalu's tribal gathering."

"And if not?" Abigail trembled with fear as a rhythmic beat struck up, accompanied by whoops and shrieks.

"I'm certain it is," said Christopher.

But how could he be sure? She glanced about, searching the blackness for movement as the chanting and droning continued.

"Should we douse the fire?" she asked uncertainly. Without it, they'd be immersed in total darkness and yet, it was a beacon to announce to anyone watching from the cover of the woods that they were there.

"No. We'll leave the fire. Trust me, the singing is part of a celebration, not an intention to attack. And anyway," he said with a smile, "if they're planning an attack, at least you'll be safe."

"How so?"

"The natives won't touch someone with a Dolphin's Kiss."

Was he teasing? Surely, he wouldn't be so cruel. But his expression appeared to be genuine.

"You believe this may protect us?" she asked, still not convinced.

"Well, it will protect you! I don't have one!" He was smiling now, and she knew he was teasing her.

Abigail relaxed slightly. If he thought they were in danger, he would be anything but playful.

"I could hold your hand and protect you," she said extending her left hand towards his. Would he flinch? Would he pull his hand away? Would his face register distaste? If he didn't react at all, then she'd know he really didn't find it unpleasant. And for some reason, that seemed vitally important.

This is most unseemly, her tiny, inner voice said although she thought it appeared to be holding its breath too as she allowed her fingers to brush the back of his hand.

He raised his eyes to look at hers and then smiled.

Encouraged, she covered his hand with hers, the Dolphin's Kiss now visible in the firelight.

He traced the outline of the dolphin with a fingertip. "Well, between us, we have a Dolphin's Kiss and a knife. Who would dare to trouble us tonight?"

"I fear I've caused trouble on this trip." Abigail changed the subject and drew her hand away. She'd hoped he wouldn't pull away from her, but she hadn't thought further than that. And certainly, she hadn't expected him to stroke her hand. Her heart pounded like the far-off drums. Well, she had no one to blame but herself. Once again, she'd been foolishly impulsive.

He smiled at her; that lop-sided, half-amused and half...... what? She couldn't decide but it made the breath catch in her throat. How could something as simple as a smile have such an effect on her? She wondered what it would be like to trace the outline of his lips with her fingertip. Would she find some clue as to why she was finding it so hard to breathe and her stomach seemed to have melted?

"Eat!" Christopher said, holding out her leaf, "It may not be so appetising when it's cold."

Abigail took the leaf with both hands, relieved that it prevented her from leaning forward and touching his mouth. What was it about this man that made her lose all reason? Whatever it was, she must find the strength to ignore it, and the best way to begin would be to stop staring at him. Thankfully, he got up and she couldn't see his face as he began to add more wood to the fire.

Abigail focused on the meat, concentrating on eating it, trying to forget what it had looked like when it had been hanging from Djalu's belt. It was smoky and rather tough, but she was hungry and wished there had been more.

"I realise this isn't quite what you're used to," Christopher said, sitting down next to her again. Closer this time.

"No, please don't apologise! You've been most considerate and treated me with more courtesy than I deserve. I confess, I'm struggling somewhat as to know how to behave. Usually, I follow society's rules, although I imagine you might find that hard to believe, considering my recent lack of good judgement."

"Well," he said slowly, "this is the Hawkesbury and there are two societies – the native tribes who've lived here forever, and the new settlers. Other than what Djalu has told me, I have little idea about the native rules. And from what I've seen, many of the new settlers, like Bartholomew Graham, are not people who adhere to rules anyway. So, it might be best if we either pretend there are none or if we need some, we could make up our own. Of course, as soon as we return to Sydney, society's usual laws and regulations will apply."

He looked at her questioningly as if he wasn't sure she'd agree. But what he'd said made sense. So far, he'd shown himself to be an honourable man. It was now obvious he'd been in an impossible position where he'd tried to keep the promise that he'd made to her and the one he'd made to Lottie – a situation that he'd tried to handle with the utmost diplomacy – until she'd foolishly leapt out of her hiding place. A dishonourable man wouldn't have cared if he'd let either of them down.

Throughout the entire journey, despite having hidden on his boat and imposed herself on him, Christopher had been courteous. Polite, yet remote. On several occasions, she'd noticed him watching her, but his expression was almost troubled as if he had many worries that pulled him this way and that. She hoped with all her heart she hadn't added to those problems.

But she hadn't once felt he would treat her with anything other than kindness and respect. She'd have to trust that whatever he did was intended to keep them both safe and she eagerly allowed the weight of guilt to roll away.

Abigail hadn't intended to play this extraordinary game of Blind Man's Buff where the removal of the blindfold revealed a world so curious that she could scarcely believe she wasn't dreaming. But now, there was nothing she could do about it – she had no choice but to remain close to this fascinating, handsome man while they were on the beach. As soon as they arrived in Sydney, the rules would be reinstated, and it would be as if she'd never put on the blindfold. She'd return to her normal life – whatever that would be, and Christopher would become Mr Randall, an associate of her father.

"Your dreams," she said, "you were going to tell me about your dreams..."

Christopher offered Abigail the bottle of rum. He wasn't sure she'd take it since he had no glasses in which to pour it. On accepting it, she'd almost transferred the bottle to her right hand. Then she'd checked herself, and with her left hand, she'd held it to her lips and drunk deeply. Passing it back to him, the birthmark was visible in the firelight.

It was good she'd accepted the rum because it would warm her through, although he doubted she was used to such a strong drink. But what harm could befall her? He certainly wouldn't take advantage of her and if it dulled reality for a few hours, so much the better.

Her life would never be the same. He suspected she'd been pampered, and her parents had always resolved any problems. Now, *they* were the problems. He almost groaned aloud as he considered what that was likely to cost her.

There's nothing you can do about it, he told himself. *Take her home, make your peace with her father if you possibly can, and forget her. Your life is disastrous enough on its own. You cannot help this girl.*

He smiled and took the bottle from her, allowing his finger to brush the back of her hand, hoping she'd understand he was showing her the mark was nothing to be ashamed of.

She gasped. "No one but you has ever touched my hand before... well, not deliberately, anyway," she said, her head lowered as if so embarrassed, she couldn't meet his gaze.

He put the bottle down, then silently, took her left hand and raising it to his lips, he kissed it.

Abigail gasped again. But this time, he was sure it was with pleasure. Her lips were parted in a surprised 'O' and her eyes were shining brightly.

Stop! His inner voice warned. *Stop this foolishness now!*

But he was treating her with sympathy and understanding. How could it possibly be wrong to make someone feel good about themselves?

You can't afford to be distracted by this girl. Ignore her. There's nothing you can do for her, the voice insisted.

I could listen, he told himself, *and I could offer her some kindness. Don't do it!* The warning voice was low and menacing in his head.

Then what sort of man am I? he asked himself.

The sort of man who takes care of his sisters and allows spoilt girls to manage their own problems, the warning voice replied.

The last letter he'd received from his elder sister had informed him that the family was doing well. One of his younger sisters would soon be married and the other had gone into service in a large house. Of course, any money Christopher sent them would be useful, but his contributions were no longer crucial to their survival. And that was just as well because Thomas Moran would be furious when he learned his daughter had gone to the Hawkesbury and uncovered a secret that he'd tried to keep from her. However, that would be nothing to the storm that would be unleashed when he discovered Christopher had been the one to convey her there – albeit unwittingly – and worse, he'd spent the night alone with her. It was likely that Mr Moran would cut all business ties with him immediately. And if that happened, Christopher would lose the Hannah Elizabeth and be plunged back into poverty.

You see how much you have to lose? The voice warned him.

Indeed, I do, he silently replied, *I risk losing my humanity.*

Humanity? The voice was scornful. *Don't pretend this is an act of charity. You have feelings for the girl. Stop now before you fall in love, or you'll regret it,* the voice said and for once, Christopher had no reply. He suspected he'd already fallen.

To stop himself from staring at her, he got up and added more wood to the flames. They crackled and spat, dancing higher and brighter, throwing a yellow glow across her face. The bruise showed up lividly on her pale skin, and as he saw her expression half-fearful and half-trusting, emotions roiled inside him. This girl had captured his heart and despite his efforts and determination to remain aloof, she'd somehow penetrated his defences. Well, what did it matter? She'd never be his, so he might as well enjoy this night. It would be the only one he'd ever spend with her. And, in fact, it may work to his advantage because once they'd returned to Sydney, if he truly loved her, he'd have eyes for no one else and could once again dedicate himself to working hard. His life would be back to normal.

"So, I've told you about my dreams, but what are yours?" Christopher asked. He'd told her about his hopes of being successful and of buying more boats and hiring men to sail them so he could send money to his sisters in London. He hadn't intended to tell her about his brother, Robert, and their vow never to marry after what they'd seen of their parents' marriage, but she was so easy to talk to – and what difference would it make? It's not like she'd ever consider him as a husband. What he didn't mention was that he was heavily in debt and that on their return, Mr Moran would probably destroy his dreams without a second thought.

"I... I don't have any dreams," she finally admitted, "I feel as if I've been in a deep, dreamless sleep all my life. But I suppose now I've woken up, my dream is to help Lottie and to get to know her. I'd like to make things up to her but really..." she trailed off miserably, "I have no idea what's going to happen to me on my return.

"I will tell Papa how well you looked after me and make sure he understands you had no part in me being here. Of course, I cannot be sure he'll believe me. After all, I explained Lottie hadn't stolen my parasol, and he didn't listen to that." She sighed. "I do believe things might be easier if I fell out of the boat on the way back to Sydney and then everyone's problems would be over."

"No! Don't say that and don't even think it! I know your life seems hard now, but it won't always be that way." He knelt next to her and took her hands.

She looked up at him with a heart-breaking expression and he longed to put his arms around her and hold her close.

"How can you possibly know that?" she asked.

"Because your parents want the best for you and I'm sure everything will be resolved, eventually."

The wind was blowing stronger now and Christopher fetched blankets from the boat and piled more wood on the fire. Their world was restricted to the small area lit by the flames and behind that, the utter blackness was filled with the unfamiliar noises of the night. Insects hummed and chirruped in the bushes nearby. As they fluttered around the flames, drawn to its brightness, their shiny bodies reflected the flickering firelight. From time to time, a splash suggested a leaping fish or perhaps a small animal jumping into the water and Christopher could see Abigail glance about nervously. She would never have experienced anything like this before and he could only imagine how afraid she was. He placed one of the blankets around her shoulders and when he told her he was going to fetch more wood to build up the fire, she seized his hand.

"Please don't leave me here alone!" Her voice held a note of panic.

He didn't tell her he had no intention of going back amongst the trees for wood. The pile he'd collected earlier was on the other side of the fire. But her hand in his was so small and warm, and somehow, it seemed to belong. He sat next to her and put his arm around her shoulders and pulled her close.

I know this isn't wise, he told his inner voice, *but it's just one night. The least I can do is to protect her and make her as comfortable as is possible in the middle of nowhere, then in the morning, I'll take her home, but until then, there's nothing either of us can do other than to pass the night as best we can. Once she's home, I'll never see her again.*

His inner voice remained silent.

7

The journey home on the Hannah Elizabeth had been calmer than their outward trip, nevertheless, the seas were still choppy, and Abigail's stomach churned. The heavy sickness, however, probably had more to do with the prospect of seeing her parents when she got back to Sydney rather than the pitching and tossing of the boat.

She mentally rehearsed several speeches until the words ran meaninglessly into each other. Well, all she could do was to tell the truth and hope the right words came when she needed them. But she wouldn't tell them about the almost-kiss, the previous night. A real kiss would be unforgivable in a girl who was promised to another man, and it would need to be confessed. But an almost-kiss? No, that didn't count. Nevertheless, she thought it would be wiser not to mention it. To be certain, she closed her eyes, testing the memory.

The previous night, Christopher had put his arm around her to comfort her while they sat together and an insect, attracted by the firelight, had accidentally flown into her hair. It had become entangled, so Christopher had held her head steady with one hand and then carefully freed the creature, allowing it to escape. But he'd continued to cradle her head with one hand and then, with the other, he'd tucked the curls that he'd disturbed, behind her ear, carefully avoiding her bruise. It had been so comforting, and she'd felt so safe, she'd lain her cheek against his palm as he continued to stroke her hair. And without her being aware of how it happened, she realised his face was close to hers. She knew, because his breath was brushing her cheek and her nostrils were filled with the woody, masculine smell of him and the rum they'd been drinking. For a second, she'd closed her eyes, lost in the sensations that rippled across her face as he continued to stroke her hair and then, accidentally, their lips had touched, setting her body trembling. Immediately, he'd let her go and moved away, his face horrified, searching hers for signs of... what? Presumably, indignation or anger. But strangely, she'd merely been filled with a longing to cup his face in her hands and guide his lips back to hers so they could touch again. And not just to make brief contact, but to gently hold them together and to see what that felt like. Of course, she hadn't dared, and immediately, he'd apologised and got up and busied himself with the fire.

It had been a shockingly exquisite moment of such intensity, she longed to be back on the beach in the darkness with the chanting and haunting music of Djalu's tribe in the distance...and Christopher.

A large wave pounded the bow, sending a deluge of spray over the boat; Abigail wiped away the salty water. At least, it had brought her back to the present and banished her shameful thoughts. The sooner they arrived in Sydney the better. At least then she'd find out how her parents would punish her and what they wanted her to do in the future. One thing was certain, they'd ensure she never saw Christopher Randall again. And that thought made her stomach twist, adding to her feelings of wretchedness.

She feasted her eyes on him, taking everything in and storing it next to all the things Lottie had told her about their mother which must also be locked away. Christopher stared ahead, his feet planted firmly against the deck, rolling with the motion of the boat. She knew Djalu was watching her while she watched Christopher because she could see him out of the corner of her eye. White dots stood out on his face, the only tangible reminder of the previous night's celebration. His mournful eyes bored into her and then periodically flickered towards Christopher. Was there a warning there? What if there was? She realised that nothing could change the fact that she'd fallen in love with Christopher Randall and that she couldn't bear the thought she'd never see him again.

It was irrelevant of course. If things went well, Hugh would marry her and possibly take her away to London. And if not, then she would presumably remain a spinster in her parents' house and society would shun her. The pain of never seeing Christopher again sliced so deeply, she wanted to open her mouth and scream into the wind.

CHAPTER EIGHT

Abigail saw her father's men waiting on the quayside well before the Hannah Elizabeth docked. Their distinctive yellow livery was recognisable against the drab browns and greys of the working men. So, Papa knew where she'd been and had sent his carriage to take her home. Well, of course, he knew. The men who'd delivered his building supplies would have told him she'd been on the quay one minute and gone the next. Papa would have worked out the rest.

Surprisingly, Christopher insisted on accompanying her to Westervale Hall. However, while he was speaking to the custom's official and she was waiting for him on the quayside, Djalu strode towards her.

"You not be the woman for Christopher." His curls trembled as he shook his head. "Christopher has woman already."

A stab of jealousy sliced through her. It was unreasonable but she couldn't help it, she felt as though Djalu had physically attacked her. So, Christopher had a woman. Well, who was she to criticise? She was promised to another man. She had no right to feel betrayed. She had no right to anything, and if she was never going to see him again, it was better the time started now. Hadn't he warned her that they were stepping outside of the rules of society while they were alone on the beach but the instant they set foot in Sydney, normal life would resume?

"Christopher has all the woman he needs." Djalu turned and pointed at the boat. "He has Hannah Elizabeth."

Relief flooded through Abigail. It wasn't a woman; it was the boat.

"Christopher make promise." Djalu placed his fist over his heart. "He never marry. Hannah Elizabeth is his woman."

"Be off with you!" One of Papa's men stepped forward to threaten Djalu. "Is he bothering you, miss?"

Abigail assured him she was well. However, Djalu had finished telling her what was on his mind and had walked off, back to the boat.

It's nothing to me, she told herself. It's not like we were ever destined to be together. We have no future. We don't even have a past – just a few hours that seemed to exist outside of time and therefore didn't count. No, she needed to close her mind to him.

"It's not necessary that you accompany me, Mr Randall." Abigail kept her voice level and her face impassive, making it clear their earlier closeness was over when he'd finished with the customs official and joined her.

He paused as if she'd struck him, then matching her formality, he said, "I rather feel, Miss Moran, that it would be churlish of me not to face your father and whatever he may decide."

Seated in her father's carriage, Abigail kept as far from Christopher as she could. She avoided looking at him during the short ride home, suppressing her tears. Briefly, on a beach in the middle of nowhere, she'd experienced something magical. But it had been an illusion, born of the darkness and wondrous surroundings – and, of course, Christopher. It had vanished like smoke as if it had never been. She now wished she'd been brave enough to pull Christopher to her and to kiss him – to taste his lips and to see where it led because at least she'd have the memory. There wouldn't have been repercussions because how could anyone be held responsible for an illusion?

Abigail nervously led Christopher into Papa's study where her parents were standing together behind his desk; stiff, upright and grim-faced. She certainly didn't expect a tearful reunion. But she was surprised to see they weren't angry at all. In their faces, she saw confusion, betrayal and uncertainty. Perhaps not entirely unexpected, as they were the emotions that jostled for attention in Abigail's mind.

Christopher stepped forward, shook Papa's hand, and bowed to Mama. "Sir, may I humbly beg your pardon for—"

Papa held up his hand to silence him, then clearing his throat and running a finger under his collar, he signalled for everyone to sit – he and Mama on one side of his desk and Abigail and Christopher on the other.

"Mr Randall, this is a delicate situation and I feel it may be counterproductive to delve too deeply into the past..." Papa's voice held none of the usual composure and confidence, and he and Mama exchanged glances.

"Despite our attempts to protect you, Abigail, you have found out everything." Papa's voice was flat and emotionless. "Now, the question is, what we do about it? Your mother and I were under the misapprehension that no one knew about your... er... start in life. But it appears that amongst a certain section of Sydney's lower classes, it is a well-known – and mercifully – well-guarded fact. Amongst those of our own class, I believe that other than my friend, Robert Bower, who first brought you to us, no one knows, and we are keen to keep it that way. The proposed marriage to Mr Hanville has been called off. So now, there are two possible courses of action. First, we all return to England and start again in a city away from London. Manchester, perhaps. Or even Edinburgh."

Papa paused and Abigail wanted to cry. It would mean he'd have to give up the house he'd built and now loved so much, as well as the standing he had in the community. Mama stared blindly ahead but Abigail could see the tears gathering in her eyes and her lower lip trembling. She didn't have as much to lose as Papa, but any ground she'd made up in gaining a place in society after the announcement of Abigail and Hugh's marriage would be lost and she'd also have to start again in a city where she knew no one.

Everyone's eyes were on Papa waiting for the second proposition.

Finally, Papa spoke, "I have an alternative solution that I believe is more acceptable to everyone. Sooner or later, it will become known that my daughter spent the night with you, Mr Randall... Her reputation will be ruined... unless, of course, she marries with great haste." He fixed Christopher with an unblinking stare.

Abigail gasped. Surely Papa wasn't putting pressure on a man who'd vowed he'd never marry? But her father was staring intently at Christopher, waiting for an answer.

Why should Christopher pay? That wasn't fair! Before she could think, Abigail had blurted out, "No, Papa! Please no!"

"Enough! Abigail, go to your room! You have caused untold damage to this family with your meddling, and I must consider how it can possibly be mended. I shall discuss that with Mr Randall alone."

Mama accompanied Abigail to her room in condemnatory silence.

"I'm sorry, Mama."

"Why do you always have to act without thinking first, Abigail?" The despair in her mother's voice was more distressing than her anger would have been.

"I truly am sorry."

"Sadly, it's too late for remorse, Abigail. Papa will settle the family's fate tonight. We must all accept whatever he decides."

Mama walked slowly back to her room and Abigail suspected she was about to suffer one of her headaches. Indeed, she could feel one coming on herself.

Molly was smoothing the cover on the bed. "Well, you certainly stirred the pot, miss! But what a lucky escape!"

"Molly, I'm tired. I don't wish to discuss anything. I merely want to go to bed." She cuddled Shadow, who wriggled with pleasure in her arms.

"Of course, miss. But if I can just say, I'd never have thought it of Mr Hanville. He's so handsome. He seemed so nice. It's hard to believe he's done them things they say he's done."

Despite herself, Abigail asked what she was talking about and Molly was determined to share her gossip.

"It were that woman what was once your wet-nurse. She came and told your mama what Mr Hanville's been getting up to since he came back to Sydney."

"I didn't know he was back."

"He got into a fight in Parramatta and had to leave. But since he's been back in Sydney, he's run up a few gambling debts and the governor's asked his men to investigate him. He's... well... he's trouble. But the less said about that, the better."

"What do you mean?" Abigail couldn't believe it. Trust Molly to make something out of nothing.

But Molly hadn't finished. "Well, the girls. Some o' them aren't in good shape."

"Which girls?" Sometimes, Abigail found it hard to follow Molly's explanations.

"The girls he entertained – if you get my meaning. He ain't no gentleman, that's for sure. Not if all the things he did to 'em were true. Shocking it was."

Abigail looked at her in horror, her skin creeping. So, it wasn't as she'd assumed that Hugh had heard of her night away in the Hawkesbury and had called the wedding off, it had been her parents who'd saved her from marriage to a cruel rake. He'd simply been after her for Papa's money? Well, of course, he had. The marriage would have been beneficial to both parties, it was a business transaction, but in her naivete, she'd assumed they'd be happy together. She thought back to the times they'd met and to the occasions when she'd wondered if she'd imagined those stunning blue eyes becoming hard and scheming, like shards of glass. Molly was right, she'd had a lucky escape.

But now, Papa was trying to force Christopher into marrying her to save her reputation. No matter that she'd hidden on his boat without his permission or knowledge, or that he'd promised never to marry. How right Djalu had been when he'd pronounced her 'trouble'. She'd brought nothing but grief to Christopher. Would Papa threaten to take his business elsewhere? Would he warn his friends to avoid Christopher too? And if so, what would happen to Christopher's dreams of a successful business?

Once Molly had gone, Abigail allowed Shadow to curl up next to her on the bed and she wept. She'd had no intention of hurting anybody, but it didn't matter what she did, somebody suffered as a result.

The following morning at breakfast, Papa announced she was to be married to Christopher Randall. Mama was still in bed and Abigail suspected she'd most likely stay there all day. She wondered if she might go back to bed too and pull the bedcovers over her head and ignore the world. How Christopher must despise her.

"A most remarkable man is Mr Randall," Papa said, "In fact, he reminds me of myself as a young man, although, I must admit, to begin with, I was rather disappointed he wasn't as prosperous as he'd led me to believe. I expected him to use the situation to his advantage, but I was wrong – very wrong."

"What do you mean, Papa?"

"Mr Randall made certain demands, but I have accepted them all. He will marry you as soon as the ceremony can be arranged and give you his name. However, he's adamant he won't accept a penny from me. I told him I couldn't have my daughter living in a boarding house and he agreed, so I will lend him the money to purchase a house. However, he has insisted he'll repay me. Such a stubborn man. But those were his terms. I must admit, I'm delighted with the outcome even though I'd hoped for someone with a better pedigree. But under the circumstances, this is the best we can do. I fear moving back to England to start again would have broken your mother's heart."

So, once again a marriage had been arranged without any input from her. But this time, with no effort on her part, it seemed Fortune had been on her side. The arrangement would mean she'd keep her reputation and gain her own household. Christopher, on the other hand, would have to break his vow to remain single, acquire debt he didn't need and a wife he didn't want.

The wedding had been lavish and even Governor Bligh had attended with his daughter, Mary.

"Such a beautiful ceremony," Anne Ferguson said, "but such a surprise that you've found a second bridegroom at such short notice when the rest of us poor ladies can scarcely find one. Not that I blame you for refusing that dreadful Hugh Hanville. What a lucky escape for you. I've heard that his name has been linked with so many scandals, one can scarcely keep up with the latest. Now, you simply must introduce me to your new husband. How handsome he is. Does he have any family in Sydney?"

"That is a truly magnificent gown," her sister, Louisa, trilled, "the embroidery is exquisite, and it matches your gloves so beautifully."

Abigail smiled and thanked her, but sadness welled up inside. The one person she'd really wanted at her wedding was Lottie, but of course, that wouldn't have been possible. And having once promised she'd find more custom for Lottie, there was now no point telling anyone who'd done the beautiful embroidery, because she was miles away along the Hawkesbury River. The feeling of emptiness grew each time someone complimented her on the beautiful gown that Lottie had embellished for her marriage to Hugh.

Everyone had wanted to meet Christopher, and to Abigail's surprise, he was genial and friendly to the guests, courteous and attentive to her and polite and deferential to her parents. The perfect bridegroom – although she alone knew it was a performance. It all contributed to giving the appearance of respectability and normality. And it seemed to be working. After a while, even Abigail wondered if perhaps now the day had come, Christopher had reconciled himself to the union.

During the few days before the ceremony, Abigail had been caught up in the excitement. Mama had never been so happy and that had made Papa happy too. Perhaps, finally, the pattern of bringing misery to people's lives might be broken and she might bring joy.

But that night, after her polite but distant husband had shown her around her new home and introduced her to Sarah, the maid, and Mrs Oliver the cook, he explained that he would return to settle the household accounts once a week when his journeys allowed. Then, he politely bade her farewell and left for his room in the boarding house. Abigail was too shocked to speak.

Shadow curled up next to her on the bed that night.

Her mother's explanation of what would take place on her wedding night had been vague. 'You'll get used to it,' had suggested something unpleasant would take place that over time would become less distasteful. But perhaps her mother's obscure comment had been right, albeit for the wrong reason. Abigail supposed that one day, she would get used to this lonely new world. She had Christopher's name and she was mistress of her own house, but he'd made it plain that although he'd provide for her, his interest in her stopped there.

Her parents had saved face and could continue to live in their beautiful home, Papa had written to Lottie to say he'd be happy for her to return to her previous position at Mrs Hippesley's and Christopher's business was growing since Papa had recommended him to various friends. Of course, Christopher had to put up with a wife he didn't want, but other than the occasional visit to ensure she had sufficient funds to run the house, he could ignore her and carry on as if he were a bachelor. If the price of so many people's happiness was her own loneliness, then so be it.

"At least I've got you," she whispered through her tears into Shadow's coat.

CHAPTER NINE

Life settled into a rhythm. Sarah was nothing like the bold and disrespectful Molly and she managed her chores well, while Mrs Oliver kept herself busy in the kitchen. At first, the cook objected to Djalu sleeping there overnight while he was ashore, but, during the weeks after the wedding, he somehow managed to charm her and it became obvious that her grumblings were half-hearted.

"That blessed savage can be quite useful at times and it's good to know there's a man in the house when Master's not here.' Was probably the most complimentary she'd ever be about him but at least, there was peace in the kitchen.

'When Master's not here,' was mostly all the time. Weekly, as promised, he'd visit to check Abigail and the house, but he was never alone with her, always assuring that Mrs Oliver attended the meetings too. Abigail noticed glances between Sarah and Mrs Oliver each time Christopher took his leave shortly after his arrival. It would be obvious to them both that he never spent any time with her – day or night.

Mama called occasionally and took tea but if she suspected her daughter's marriage was in name only, she didn't refer to it.

Mrs Ferguson visited with her daughters. Anne had recently become engaged to George Valance, an officer in the New South Wales Corps and was keen to let Abigail know her good fortune.

"And your papa is going to build us a fine house," she said glancing around Abigail's drawing room, her nose wrinkling, as if to say hers would be far grander than Abigail's.

"Although this is simply splendid," Louisa said quickly, "and how gratified you must be that Mr Randall's services are so in demand."

"What do you know about business, Louisa?" Anne asked, her eyebrows raised in derision.

"Well, probably more than you! At least I listen to what's going on around me! Unlike you, who can only make doe eyes at George!"

"Such nonsense!"

"Really? Well, I know Mr Randall now has two men working for him on his other boat and I do believe he's looking for a third boat. There!" Louisa looked triumphant.

'Now, now, girls! What will Mrs Randall think of you squabbling so? And Louisa, there is no merit in such information. Girls do not need to know about commerce, it is unbecoming." Mrs Ferguson snapped her fan shut and wagged it like a finger at her younger daughter.

Anne sucked in her cheeks and sent her sister a gleeful glance. Ordinarily, Abigail would have thought of something soothing to cool the situation and save Louisa's face, but her mind was reeling. Christopher had a new boat and more men? He was looking for a third boat? And she'd heard this from the sister of a girl who couldn't even be considered a friend.

"I'm sure you must be most gratified at your husband's success," Anne said.

Abigail wouldn't allow herself to reveal the strange nature of her marriage, so she smiled and swallowed back her tears. As she did so, a cake crumb caught in her throat, and she was saved further comment or questioning by a bout of coughing. To Abigail's great relief, Mrs and the Misses Ferguson left shortly after.

As soon as Djalu returned, she would question him. At least, in future, she'd have more idea about her husband's life even if she had to ask somebody else to find out.

Usually, Christopher sent word several days in advance to inform her when he'd been free to visit the house. She both yearned for and dreaded those days.

During the meetings, her husband showed himself to be a kind, gentle, caring man, but one who was impossibly out of her reach.

"So, is it better now?" he asked her during one of his visits.

"Erm...?" Abigail had no idea to what he was referring. He'd been tapping his bottom lip as he ran his other finger down the list of accounts, and she couldn't banish the memory of that almost-kiss when their lips had brushed and how she'd wished afterwards that she hadn't broken away.

"The kitchen chimney! Is it better now it's been cleaned?" He frowned at her. "I think that if our weekly meeting bores you, Abigail, you need only say. In fact, Mrs Oliver has proved to be more than capable. I shall leave the finances in her hands and in future, she can let Djalu know how much I owe, and I shall send the money to cover everything. Will that suit you?"

"No! Oh no! I wasn't bored, I assure you." She was horrified. If these visits stopped, she'd never see him at all.

Perhaps that might be less painful, her inner voice said.

There was a knock at the door, followed by raised voices. Sarah's indignant squeal and a man's voice continued for a few seconds until the door flew open. Sarah almost fell headlong with a startled shriek, having been shoved in the small of the back by Hugh Hanville. He stood squarely in the doorframe, dishevelled, and smelling strongly of cigar smoke and brandy.

"My, my! What a charming scene! Husband and wife in a delightful tête-à-tête." His voice was slurred, and it was obvious why he reeked of brandy. He swayed slightly but his ice-blue eyes burned with a disturbing intensity that suggested he wasn't as far gone in his drink as it appeared.

Christopher leapt to his feet. "What's the meaning of this, Hanville? How dare you burst into my house uninvited!" He strode towards the unwelcome guest, only stopping when Hugh withdrew a knife from the inside of his jacket. Sarah screamed and slipped out of the room. Shadow, with a frenzy of barking, leapt up at Hugh who aimed several kicks at him.

"Call the dog off!" Hugh shouted and Abigail screamed at Shadow to come to heel. Christopher grabbed her arm to keep her back, standing in front of her and the growling dog. Mrs Oliver rushed into the room, wiping her hands on her apron, stopping abruptly when she saw the tableau before her.

"Get over there!" Hugh indicated she should stand with the others by the fireplace. He slashed the air with the knife to herd them together. Mrs Oliver skirted the room towards the others, keeping her back to the wall. Her round eyes were fixed on Hugh's blade.

Christopher held his hands palm upwards in a placatory gesture and calmly stepped towards Hugh. Keeping his tone friendly, he said, "Hanville, let's discuss this like gentlemen—"

"Gentlemen?" sneered Hugh, "You're no gentleman, sir! And she's no lady but, she was mine until you came on the scene!" He pointed the blade at Abigail. "Her father and I had a nice arrangement. But you put an end to all that. Now, I've come to claim what's mine."

"Good grief, man! You'll have to get past me first before I allow my wife to go with you!" Christopher said.

Hugh began to laugh; his pale blue eyes were glacial. "I don't want her! I want recompense. You owe me. Moran was going to settle a fortune on his daughter. I was relying on that money, and I'll be damned if I'm going to let you get away with it. So, let's start with that..." he motioned to the leather pouch on the table that Christopher had brought to pay the household bills. "And then, I believe we might come to terms for the future."

"I'm not going to pay you one penny," Christopher said calmly.

"Oh, I think you will. Accidents happen all the time and I wouldn't like to imagine what could befall your pretty wife or her cur... you can't protect them all the time. Now, hand that money over." He lunged at Christopher who stepped aside as the blade slit the air. However, just as Hugh regained his balance and raised his arm to strike again, Djalu sprang from behind him and grabbed his arm. He'd been following Mrs Oliver but had stopped short of entering the room and had remained hidden behind the hall door. Hugh struck at him with his other hand and caught him a blow on the temple that stunned him, sending him crashing to the ground.

Christopher took the opportunity to charge at Hugh. He grabbed his wrist, trying to force him to drop the knife. Abigail screamed. The blade flashed, and with an enraged shout, Hugh threw Christopher off-balance, plunging the knife downwards. Christopher swerved, the blade narrowly missing his chest. He grasped Hugh's wrist once again. Both men crashed to the floor in a deadly embrace.

The brandy seemed to have lent Hugh superhuman strength and he and Christopher were locked together, rolling on the rug in front of the hearth. Shadow barked madly, straining to get at Hugh but Abigail held his struggling body tightly. Christopher's arms were strong but with the weight of Hugh on top of him, they began to tremble as he fought to fend off the stabbing blade.

Hugh twisted sharply, throwing Christopher off balance. Abigail screamed as he brought the knife down. Djalu struggled to his knees, shook his head as if to clear it and launched himself at Hugh, forcing the knife from his grasp and just as Christopher pushed Hugh away, two constables arrived with a red-faced and breathless Sarah.

It wasn't until the two men grabbed Hugh and hauled him up that Abigail saw the rapidly spreading bloodstain on Christopher's shirtsleeve.

When Dr Fuller, the physician, arrived he inspected, cleaned and bandaged the wound.

"Not life-threatening," he said, "but there has been a large loss of blood and the wound is so deep that if any fibres from Mr Randall's shirt are still lodged in the muscle, there is a chance of infection. Should he develop a fever, please don't hesitate to call me. And needless to say, Mr Randall must rest to hasten the healing process."

He helped Christopher upstairs and Abigail directed them to her bedroom. Despite his weakness, Christopher looked at her in alarm, but she steadily returned his gaze and said pointedly, "Thank you, Dr Fuller, I will ensure he remains in bed until he has recovered."

When the physician had gone, Christopher raised himself on his uninjured arm as if to get out of bed.

"Stop!" Abigail stood with hands on hips. "You need somebody to remain with you until we're sure you won't develop a fever. So, either you stay here, or I accompany you to your boarding house. The choice is yours!"

Christopher sank back onto the pillows, his face as white as the bed linen, and closed his eyes. His look of resignation told her he'd accepted her decision and even if he hadn't, it appeared he was too weak to leave the bed, let alone the house.

Abigail settled down in a comfortable chair that she dragged to the bedside and waited with Shadow on her lap. Mrs Oliver brought her a dish of tea in the early hours and offered to take over, but after thanking her for the drink, Abigail refused any help. It was probably too soon to tell, but so far, Christopher had not displayed any signs of fever, indeed he'd not displayed signs of much at all – he'd simply lain there motionless, his breathing shallow and eyes opening from time to time although he didn't seem to see her.

Abigail began to wonder if Dr Fuller had been mistaken. Blood had spurted out of the wound and in her panic, she'd simply watched. A scream had died in her throat as she'd realised that she had no idea what to do. It had been Djalu who'd taken over and applied pressure to Christopher's arm, staunching some of the flow until the physician arrived. Now, she silently berated herself for her ignorance and wondered if Christopher would pay the price for her inexperience. Thank goodness Djalu had regained consciousness.

Mrs Oliver eventually organised a cot to be brought into the bedroom and Abigail curled up with Shadow and slept by one side of the bed, while the cook sat in the chair by the other side, having promised faithfully to waken her mistress should she notice any change in the master.

Time lost all meaning for Abigail as she slept for an hour or two, then sat next to Christopher looking for signs of improvement but dreading the worst. For several days, he was remarkably still, his breathing weak and shallow, and his face, deathly white. However, gradually a little colour returned to his cheeks, and he took some soup without much coaxing.

"The worst is over," Mrs Oliver said confidently, her cheeks puffed with pride that Master had seemed to enjoy the soup she'd made, and when the physician returned, he confirmed that Mr Randall's progress was encouraging.

"If your husband continues to rest, Mrs Randall, I believe he'll regain all movement in his shoulder and arm."

That night, Christopher slept deeply for the first time and although it was hard to tell in the candlelight, Abigail thought his colour was returning.

The following morning, Christopher asked Djalu to go to Mrs Riley's boarding house and bring fresh clothes, tooth cloth, toothpowder and his shaving equipment from his rooms. Then he asked Sarah for hot water so he could shave and wash on Djalu's return.

Abigail knew Christopher would be leaving soon. He was probably keen to get back to work and if he wasn't strong enough, then he'd go home to the boarding house and convalesce. Sadness washed over her, leaving behind an aching emptiness.

She wanted him to be well, of course, but once again she'd be alone without the man she loved desperately. He was so kind and honourable, even stepping in front of the knife-wielding Hugh, to protect her. She owed him so much, but it was unlikely he'd ever allow her to repay him – he seemed to find her presence disagreeable. From time to time, she caught him looking intently at her and then when their eyes met, he glanced away. There was no doubt he couldn't bear to be in the same room as her.

"Christopher not strong. He not go home yet," Djalu said to Abigail, as he came out of the room, having delivered Christopher's clothes and washing items. He crossed his arms over his chest and shook his head. "Stop him," he said.

"I don't know how to stop him," Abigail admitted but he merely gestured with his hands and spoke in his own language in a way that suggested she should go into the bedroom and try.

She knocked on the door and waited until Christopher called for her to enter. He was dressed, holding his bag and coat over his uninjured arm as if ready to leave but as he walked to the door, he swayed slightly and staggered. She rushed to him and took the bag and coat. "No," she said, "don't leave. You're not strong enough. I understand you can't wait to get away from me but you're too weak to leave yet."

He sat on the bed and looked up at her in surprise. "I rather thought it was you who couldn't wait to be rid of me. My presence here is preventing you from resuming your usual life."

"I sincerely hope I didn't give you the impression you were disturbing me! You risked your life to protect me! Looking after you was the least I could do to express my gratitude!"

"Ah, you felt you had to repay a debt. Well, your nursing and your care have been more than enough and I thank you sincerely for looking after me but now, I think it best to take my leave. I expect you require time to come to terms with what must have been a dreadful shock. I can't imagine how disappointed you must be."

"Disappointed?" What did Christopher mean? Disappointed that he'd been wounded? That he didn't want to be with her? That their marriage was a sham? "W...well," she hesitated, not wanting to sound as though she was criticising, "I confess I wish things had unfolded differently—"

"Differently!" Anger burned brightly in his eyes. "The man comes into our home and attempts to rob us at knifepoint, and you wish he'd behaved differently? I knew you still had feelings for him, but your love must be strong, indeed, to overlook such behaviour!"

Abigail stepped backwards away from him, surprised by the intensity of his outburst. "I believe we must be talking at cross purposes. I have no feelings for Hugh Hanville. True, for a short while, I convinced myself I did, but I realise now that I wanted to please my parents. And, yes, I was flattered that such a man had agreed to marry me. Trust me, I cannot believe I was so naive. Deep down, even though I didn't admit it to myself, I was very wary of him, even slightly afraid. But I assure you I have no fond feelings for the man who came into your home and attempted to rob you at knifepoint. There is no 'our' and no 'us' in this household or this marriage and that is why I wish things had unfolded differently."

"Prettily said." Christopher rose and glared at her. "And yet, I wonder if the passing months haven't clouded your memory, for when your father suggested I ask for your hand, you made it clear that would not be acceptable to you. If I remember rightly, you exclaimed 'No, Papa! Please no!' in a voice so full of anguish, no one could be left in any doubt as to how offensive such a proposition would be."

"No, Christopher—"

"I heard you, Abigail. There's no point denying it. You found the prospect of marrying me unacceptable. If that isn't because you preferred Hugh Hanville, then your reluctance must have been at the thought of sharing your life with me."

"No, that wasn't it at all!"

Christopher looked at her in disbelief. "Then why were you so distressed at your father's proposition?"

Abigail stepped towards him, raised her chin and stared him in the eyes. "My distress was because my father was putting pressure on you to marry when you'd vowed never to do so. It was grossly unjust. My meddling had caused turmoil in the lives of Lottie and my parents; I couldn't bear the thought that you, an innocent bystander, had been caught up in all the chaos I'd caused. That is why I didn't want Papa to push you into something you didn't want to do. You'd been so good to me and yet he was making you pay." She shook her head sadly. "You have every reason to despise me for all the trouble I've brought you."

"I assure you, I don't despise you!" His anger was replaced by disbelief.

"Then why do you always turn away when I look at you as if you can't bear the sight of me?"

"That's not true, Abigail."

"Perhaps you'd care to tell me the truth. As soon as you leave, our meetings will revert to once a week in the presence of Mrs Oliver, and I fear I will never know what's on your mind. Why will you not look me in the eyes?"

"I... I don't want to see your dissatisfaction. I do my best, Abigail. I gave you my name and I provide for all your needs, but you always seem discontented. I've tried to give you what you want but, I admit, I'm at a loss..."

She stared at him. How could she tell this man who'd given up so much for her that she wanted the one thing he couldn't give her? She craved his love.

He looked at her enquiringly, waiting for a response. But the words wouldn't come. It was useless begging him to love her. It was obviously not in him to do so.

He nodded curtly as if coming to a decision, then sank wearily onto the bed and held his head in his hands. "I understand that you find the constraints of our marriage intolerable and if being married to me is so offensive, then I have a solution. If both parties agree the marriage has not been consummated, then we can apply for an annulment. I expect your parents will resist such measures, but they cannot stop it if that's what you want. You will be blameless. And if you need me to admit to committing adultery, then I will claim whatever you like in order to get your freedom."

"No! How can you even suggest that?"

He raked his fingers through his hair and looked at her in confusion.

"Then please..." There was a catch in his voice. "Tell me what it is you want. I will do whatever you ask."

"I fear," said Abigail wringing her hands, "that's not possible."

"Please humour me and tell me what it is that you want – that you believe I cannot give you. If you're correct, then what have you lost? I can arrange to meet Mrs Oliver when you are out, and you will never need to see me again. But consider this...Perhaps you are wrong in your assumptions..."

"Sit please," he said pulling the chair on which she'd sat during her vigil, next to where he was seated on the bed. "If this is to be the last time we speak face-to-face then let us at least have one last honest conversation. Tell me about yourself. Tell me what brought us to this point. Speak to me!"

So, this may well be her final meeting alone with her husband.

Abigail sighed and began, "There's so much to explain." She paused and tried to put her thoughts in order. "First, I'd like to tell you about my parents. Mrs Riley visited me a few weeks ago and I think I now come close to understanding many things that puzzled me as I was growing up. You may be shocked by Papa's willingness to pay you to marry me. Of course, no father wants his daughter's reputation ruined and after our time away alone in the Hawkesbury, my reputation was sorely at risk. But my parents' desire for me to marry goes back further than that. Mrs Riley told me that just after my parents adopted me, a servant predicted that, 'Bad blood would out' and that I would ultimately behave in a scandalous way because I'm the child of a convict prostitute. Mama tried to keep me under control, but I was a wayward child, always behaving impulsively and testing limits. Mama feared that if she was too strict, I'd push even harder against her, and she'd lose any control she had. But I lived my life believing I didn't measure up to their ideals. In truth, they were more afraid of what I might do in the future, rather than anything I'd done – until I hid on your boat, of course. Papa was desperate to marry me off before I spoiled any chances of finding a husband. And as desperate as that sounds, he liked you – he's come to think of you like a son. And he thought you'd look after me. He was right, of course..."

"That's all very interesting, Abigail, but I'm still no closer to knowing how you feel."

Tell him, said her inner voice. *You have nothing to lose.*

Except for my dignity, she silently replied.

Dignity or stubbornness? Her inner voice asked. *Do not lose this last opportunity. You usually rush headlong into things without thinking. Do that now!*

Abigail blurted out, her eyes blazing, "You want to know how I feel? Well, I find myself married to a man with whom I've fallen deeply in love. Sadly, my love is not returned. There, that's the heart of the matter. Are you now satisfied?"

He stared at her for several seconds and she looked down at her hands, too embarrassed to meet his gaze. Well, what did it matter what he thought of her now? She would never see him again. The annulment could go ahead although she would never accuse him of adultery.

"But how can that be?" he asked softly.

"Is it of any account?"

"It is of great account... particularly if I feel the same."

She looked up sharply. Was he mocking her?

"And I do feel the same," he said leaning forward to take her hand.

"I can't believe you feel anything other than resentment towards me. Just as you remember my comments when I realised Papa wanted you to marry me, so I noticed your face in that same instant, and I saw distaste, as if the idea was repugnant."

"No, not repugnant. Never that. Your father caught me by surprise. I must admit, at first, I wasn't happy, not because I didn't want you, but because of your father's terms. He offered me a large dowry and substantial financial incentives..."

"But I don't understand. Most men would be pleased—"

"I am not most men, Abigail! I thought more of you than that! Much more. You're not a commodity to be bought or sold; to be bartered over like a sheep! That's why I will pay your father back every penny I owe him. I'm grateful to him for recommending my packet service to his influential friends but I have accepted no favours other than the greatest he could give me – his daughter."

Could this man be telling the truth? Was it possible he'd been reluctant to marry her because he hadn't wanted to benefit financially? Yes, she decided – knowing him as she did – she could believe that. And he'd avoided her because he'd thought she'd wanted Hugh Hanville. So, he'd paid for her to live in luxury while he worked hard to pay off the debts she incurred and all the while, allowing her the freedom to do as she pleased.

How ironic that all she'd wanted was to be his wife and to love him.

"Then... then, you feel the same about me as I do about you? How can that be?" she asked in wonder.

"I refused to admit it to myself, but I fell in love with you that night we spent alone in the Hawkesbury," Christopher said.

"And I believe that's when I fell in love with you too. Perhaps," she added with a sad smile, "we should have stayed on that beach. Something started that night and it stopped as soon as we began the journey home."

He caught hold of her hands. "Then, let's go back! No," he added quickly, "not in reality, just in our imaginations. We created a special world there and if we had it once, then we must be able to find it again."

"But how?"

"Come, sit next to me." He settled her next to him on the bed.

"And now?" she asked, feeling very shy.

"Shh!" he said, placing a finger against her lips. "Now, close your eyes and listen. Can you hear the river running by? And the sound of Djalu and his tribe in the distance? How about the leaves rustling above us?"

She nodded.

"We sat next to each other in the darkness and shared our lives." He leaned his forehead on hers. "Can we go back and start again?"

"There is a matter that wasn't resolved," she said. "We shared an almost-kiss and I've wondered so often since then what might have happened had it been a real kiss."

"Let's find out." He smiled and taking her left hand, he raised it to his lips." For a second, she was disappointed wondering if he was merely going to kiss her hand, yet she was touched that he'd chosen the hand with the birthmark. He turned her hand over and kissed her palm, then each fingertip in turn, all the while with his eyes fixed on hers. He continued planting kisses up her arm until he reached the puffed sleeve of her dress which he slid off her shoulder and continued kissing the tender skin of her neck. She threw her head back, lost in the sensations that radiated from wherever his lips touched.

Finally, he reached her mouth. Tentatively at first, he kissed her, then as she put her arms around his neck and pulled him closer, it deepened until she felt as though she were drowning in pleasure.

Several days later, Christopher insisted on walking to the wharf to supervise the loading of his boat. He'd accepted he wasn't yet fit enough to sail because although his shoulder was healing well, it hadn't regained full strength. Djalu kept him informed about the men he'd hired and told him they were all working hard.

"Come to the quay with me, Abby." Christopher stood patiently, neck extended while she tied his stock.

"I rather think you could tie this yourself! Your shoulder is better now." She squealed as he slid his hands around her waist and pulled her close.

"Well, yes, I believe I could do it myself but where would be the fun in that? Tying a stock is rather dull in comparison to..."

"Christopher! Stop! I thought you wanted to see your boat."

"I do! I do! It's just that I find you so very distracting." He nuzzled her neck.

"Christopher! If you want me to come, I must dress and you're not helping."

"Yes, you're quite right." He checked his pocket watch and nodded in a business-like fashion. "And it's important that you come with me today. I want to show you something."

Abigail was aware that now Christopher had moved in with her, the household was a happier place. The silence that had hung heavily in each room since she'd become its mistress had lifted and even Djalu now seemed to accept her. Christopher had told her that as a native in a white settlement, Djalu recognised his position was precarious and that if Christopher's business had failed no one would be likely to employ him. It was therefore important to him that the business, and indeed, the Hannah Elizabeth remained afloat. Djalu had known why Christopher had decided not to marry and when he spotted his master's attraction to Abigail, he'd considered her an unwelcome complication who could only cause trouble. However now, the packet business appeared to be thriving and Djalu had become reconciled to the idea of Christopher having married. On several occasions when Abigail had been in town, she'd seen Djalu with a young native woman and she wondered if perhaps he was thinking about settling down too.

Finally, Abigail was dressed and ready to go. She called Shadow, picking him up and carrying him out into the street. Christopher took her arm and led her towards the wharf where he wanted to check up on the men he'd recently employed. Abigail could barely catch her breath she was so full of pride for her husband. His success had been achieved by his hard work and determination, and not because of any assistance that her father had offered. And more than that, Christopher had risked his business because he didn't want to use her as a bargaining chip. She wondered how she'd have felt if he'd agreed to her father's terms. Would she always have wondered if Christopher valued his boat and business more than her? Now, at least she knew that was not the case.

"There! Do you see it, Abigail?" Christopher asked, pointing along the quay.

She peered along the line of vessels that were moored in the wharf. Men clambered up rigging and swarmed over the decks and quayside, carrying barrels, boxes, baskets and bags, however, she couldn't see the Hannah Elizabeth amongst them. Perhaps it was hidden behind the larger boat at the far end.

Unexpectedly, Christopher stopped to speak to several men who were loading bricks onto a boat much larger than the Hannah Elizabeth. He was speaking to them as if he knew all about their cargo and she realised this was one of Christopher's new boats. She gasped when she saw its name – Abigail's Pride

Christopher broke away from the man who continued loading goods onto the boat and smiled at her. "Do you like it?"

"Oh yes!"

"Come," he said holding out his hand, "come and see my other boat." He carried on towards the vessel behind which Abigail had supposed the Hannah Elizabeth was hiding.

"See!" On the prow was painted the name Dolphin's Pride. Tears pricked Abigail's eyes. She'd expected to feel satisfaction at seeing the evidence of Christopher's success but hadn't thought to be included in any way. Now, a crew sailed on one boat bearing her name and although very few would know, the other boat was named in celebration of her Dolphin's Kiss.

"You haven't sold the Hannah Elizabeth, have you?" she asked in alarm. He'd done so well in such a short time that he could hardly have afforded to buy two large vessels without selling the boat he'd named for his mother.

"No, I still have her. She's expected shortly."

"But how have you managed to afford two large boats and yet still kept the Hannah Elizabeth?"

"Ah, well, with all the new settlers along the Hawkesbury, several men were keen to invest in the packet trade. I suspect your father drew their attention to the great opportunity and I'm very grateful because it meant I could expand my business but still keep the Hannah Elizabeth." He paused and craned his neck to look out into the cove. "I had hoped she'd be here by now, but she must have been delayed."

He screwed up his eyes against the harsh sunlight that glinted on the water. "Is that her?" He pointed towards a boat that had just appeared around the point. "I do believe it is. Shall we wait?"

Abigail nodded, recalling the last time she'd been on the quay and how frightening it had appeared. Men shouting and jostling, pushing carts and rolling barrels. Now, however, on the arm of her husband, it was more interesting than alarming. She twirled her parasol. Every so often, a cloud drifted across the sun, giving respite from the fierce rays. The breeze coming off the water, cooled her further. Yes, it was pleasant waiting here on the wharf where her husband seemed to be well-known and respected.

The Hannah Elizabeth was making good time and was soon close enough for her to make out the faces of Christopher's men. Abigail stared in disbelief, for one of the people on the Hannah Elizabeth was a woman – a woman she recognised so well, it was as if she was peering into a mirror. It was Lottie. Abigail looked up at Christopher. He smiled down at her.

"Happy?" he asked.

Abigail couldn't speak. She swallowed trying to force words past the lump in her throat.

Lottie waved shyly and Abigail thought her heart would burst with happiness.

CHAPTER TEN

Jane Moran reached out, and with a tentative finger, she stroked the downy head of the sleeping baby.

Her granddaughter.

Delphine Jane Randall.

An odd name to be sure, but Abigail had explained it was quite à la mode in France. Although why a child would be given a French name or one that was associated with dolphins, Jane couldn't conceive.

She looked up at Thomas and saw the tears in his eyes. Emotion choked him and he couldn't speak. She was similarly affected. This tender moment exceeded their dreams.

The arrival of the child had been unexpected, coming a week earlier than Dr Fuller had predicted. But after the irregular beginning of Abigail and Christopher's marriage, it was a wonder a child had come at all. Jane had been most concerned after the wedding when it appeared that her new son-in-law was rarely home – and worse, he'd kept his rented room in a boarding house. At first, she'd assumed he had a mistress, but Thomas assured her he wouldn't have had time for another woman as he worked such long hours. Her husband had been most impressed with the young man and that had been good enough for Jane.

Delphine clutched with tiny, plump fingers at the shawl in which she was wrapped. It was exquisitely made; lace with beading work and a prayer for the child embroidered in one corner. The baby's Aunt Charlotte had made it although if anyone of quality asked Jane, she would say it came from Hippesley's Emporium, rather than to draw attention to the relationship between her beloved granddaughter and Lottie Jackson – or Charlotte as Jane insisted she was known. Well, it was only a slight twist of the truth. Thomas had discreetly brought Charlotte back to Sydney, giving her a sum of money as recompense. The girl had intended to purchase a small shop where she planned to sell lace and embroidered items, however, Mrs Hippesley – always a woman with her eye on a profit, had persuaded Charlotte to buy into her shop instead, and now, she was a junior partner in Hippesley's Emporium.

To her credit, the girl worked hard and even Jane had to admit, she had a certain dignity not usually seen in one of the lower classes.

She'd tried to persuade Abigail against inviting Charlotte to the christening but typically, her daughter had insisted on her own way, although Jane had been relieved to see Charlotte had behaved modestly at the ceremony, not drawing attention to herself and she'd slipped away early from the lavish party Jane had organised. The gathering was the only thing that Jane had insisted on and for once, Abigail had given way.

Before Charlotte had left, Mrs Ferguson had pointed her out with her lorgnette and enquired, "And who is that fashionably dressed young lady over there?"

Another guest had cut in before Jane could reply, "My dear! That is Miss Charlotte Jackson! Surely you've heard of her exquisite lace and embroidery! It is absolutely *de rigueur* to ask for her when one is seeking a stylish ensemble in Hippesley's Emporium. I believe she's a close acquaintance of Mrs Randall. Mrs Moran, you must be acquainted with her too?"

"Oh, yes," Jane had agreed.

"How simply marvellous! I wonder if you would introduce me to her…" another lady said and while the conversation about the latest fashions from France continued, Jane resolved to encourage the relationship between the fashionable young woman and her daughter – and, of course, her beloved granddaughter.

Delphine flexed her hand and Jane nervously touched the tiny palm. The baby closed her fist around her grandmother's finger. Delicate skin, so white and pure and no sign of any marks. Jane had checked when Abigail wasn't looking. Not that it had mattered to Abigail in the end. Christopher adored his wife with or without a birthmark. Neither had the mark been a harbinger of the wantonness Jane had once feared would come from sharing the tainted blood of a prostitute mother. Abigail had once been too impetuous for her own good but had never displayed lewdness. Charlotte also behaved with propriety and decency, so perhaps there was no truth in those words the cook had uttered all those years ago that, 'Bad blood will out'. Thomas had told her it was nonsense and it seemed he was right. She wished she'd taken note of his words years ago. But he'd always had more knowledge than her.

Delphine opened her eyes and looked up at her grandmother. Jane's breath caught in her throat at such perfection.

"Happy, my love? Thomas finally managed to speak. He placed a hand on her shoulder and looking up at him she nodded. Life had been good, despite her always fearing the worst. She'd spent Abigail's lifetime fighting with shadows. But she wouldn't need to do that for this child because Delphine had a blessed life ahead of her. Yes, Jane decided, she would make sure of that.

***

If you enjoyed this story, please consider leaving a review on Amazon. For information about other books in this series, please go to https://dawnknox.com and sign up for the newsletter. Thank you.

About the Author

Dawn spent much of her childhood making up stories filled with romance, drama and excitement. She loved fairy tales, although if she cast herself as a character, she'd more likely have played the part of the Court Jester than the Princess. She didn't recognise it at the time, but she was searching for the emotional depth in the stories she read. It wasn't enough to be told the Prince loved the Princess, she wanted to know how he felt and to see him declare his love. She wanted to see the wedding. And so, she'd furnish her stories with those details.

Nowadays, she hopes to write books that will engage readers' passions. From poignant stories set during the First World War to the zany antics of the inhabitants of the fictitious town of Basilwade; and from historical romances, to the fantasy adventures of a group of anthropomorphic animals led by a chicken with delusions of grandeur, she explores the richness and depth of human emotion.

A book by Dawn will offer laughter or tears – or anything in between, but if she touches your soul, she'll consider her job well done.

You can follow her here on https://dawnknox.com
Amazon Author Central: mybook.to/DawnKnox
on Facebook: https://www.facebook.com/DawnKnoxWriter
on Twitter: https://twitter.com/SunriseCalls
on Instagram: https://www.instagram.com/sunrisecalls/
on YouTube: shorturl.at/luDNQ

The Duchess of Sydney
The Lady Amelia Saga – Book One

Betrayed by her family and convicted of a crime she did not commit, Georgiana is sent halfway around the world to the penal colony of Sydney, New South Wales. Aboard the transport ship, the Lady Amelia, Lieutenant Francis Brooks, the ship's agent becomes her protector, taking her as his "sea-wife" – not because he has any interest in her but because he has been tasked with the duty.

Despite their mutual distrust, the attraction between them grows. But life has not played fair with Georgiana. She is bound by family secrets and lies. Will she ever be free again – free to be herself and free to love?

Order from Amazon: mybook.to/TheDuchessOfSydney
Paperback: ISBN: 9798814373588
eBook: ASIN: B09Z8LN4G9

The Finding of Eden
The Lady Amelia Saga – Book Two

1782 – the final year of the Bonner family's good fortune. Eva, the eldest child of a respectable London watchmaker becomes guardian to her sister, Keziah, and brother, Henry. Barely more than a child herself, she tries to steer a course through a side of London she hadn't known existed. But her attempts are not enough to keep the family together and she is wrongfully accused of a crime she didn't commit and transported to the penal colony of Sydney, New South Wales on the Lady Amelia.

Treated as a virtual slave, she loses hope. Little wonder that when she meets Adam Trevelyan, a fellow convict, she refuses to believe they can find love.

Order from Amazon: mybook.to/TheFindingOfEden
Paperback: ISBN: 9798832880396
eBook: ASIN: B0B2WFD279

The Other Place
The Lady Amelia Saga – Book Three

1790 – the year Keziah Bonner and her younger brother, Henry, exchange one nightmare for another. If only she'd listened to her elder sister, Eva, the Bonner children might well have remained together. But headstrong Keziah had ignored her sister's pleas. Eva had been transported to the far side of the world for a crime she hadn't committed and Keziah and Henry had been sent to a London workhouse. When the prospect of work and a home in the countryside is on offer, both Keziah and Henry leap at the chance. But they soon discover they've exchanged the hardship of the workhouse for worse conditions in the cotton mill. The charismatic but irresponsible nephew of the mill owner shows his interest in Keziah. But Matthew Gregory's attempts to demonstrate his feelings – however well-intentioned – invariably results in trouble for Keziah. Is Matthew yet another of Keziah's poor choices or will he be a major triumph?

Order from Amazon: mybook.to/TheOtherPlace
Paperback ISBN: 9798839521766
eBook ASIN: B0B5VPLHGQ

The Dolphin's Kiss
The Lady Amelia Saga – Book Four

Born 1790; in Sydney, New South Wales, to wealthy parents, Abigail Moran is attractive and intelligent, and other than a birthmark on her hand that her mother loathes, she has everything she could desire. Soon, she'll marry handsome, witty, Hugh Hanville. Abigail's life is perfect. Or is it? A chance meeting with a shopgirl, Lottie Jackson, sets in motion a chain of events that finds Abigail in the remote reaches of the Hawkesbury River with sea captain, Christopher Randall. He has inadvertently stumbled across the secret that binds Abigail and Lottie. Will he be able to help Abigail come to terms with the secret or will Fate keep them apart?

Order from Amazon:
Paperback: ISBN eBook: ASIN

The Pearl of Aphrodite
The Lady Amelia Saga – Book Five

1811 – At the age of twenty-four, Charlotte Jackson is neither a member of Sydney Penal Colony's high society nor one of its convicts. She yearns to belong. To be valued. So, when unscrupulous Ruth Bellamy invites her to London to set up a dressmaking business, Charlotte is easily persuaded. During the voyage, she falls in love with Alexander Melford who is also seeking a better life in London. But although Fate throws Charlotte and Alexander together, they are torn apart by the lies and deceit of those around them. Will they ever escape the deception that binds them and be free to love?

Order from Amazon
Paperback: ISBN
eBook: ASIN:

The Great War
100 Stories of 100 Words Honouring Those Who Lived And Died 100 Years Ago

  One hundred short stories of ordinary men and women caught up in the extraordinary events of the Great War – a time of bloodshed, horror and heartache. One hundred stories, each told in exactly one hundred words, written one hundred years after they might have taken place. Life between the years of 1914 and 1918 presented a challenge for those fighting on the Front, as well as for those who were left at home—regardless of where that home might have been. These stories are an attempt to glimpse into the world of everyday people who were dealing with tragedies and life-changing events on such a scale that it was unprecedented in human history. In many of the stories, there is no mention of nationality, in a deliberate attempt to blur the lines between winners and losers, and to focus on the shared tragedies. This

is a tribute to those who endured the Great War and its legacy, as well as a wish that future generations will forge such strong links of friendship that mankind will never again embark on such a destructive journey and will commit to peace between all nations.

"This is a book which everyone should read - the pure emotion which is portrayed in each and every story brings the whole of their experiences - whether at the front or at home - incredibly to life. Some stories moved me to tears with their simplicity, faith and sheer human endeavour." (Amazon)

Order from Amazon: <u>mybook.to/TheGreatWar100</u>

Paperback: ISBN 978-1532961595
eBook: ASIN B01FFRN7FW
Hardcover: ISBN 979-8413029800

THE FUTURE BROKERS
Written as DN Knox with Colin Payn

It's 2050 and George Williams considers himself a lucky man. It's a year since he—like millions of others—was forced out of his job by Artificial Intelligence. And a year since his near-fatal accident. But now, George's prospects are on the way up. With a state-of-the-art prosthetic arm and his sight restored, he's head-hunted to join a secret Government department—George cannot believe his luck.

He is right not to believe it. George's attraction to his beautiful boss, Serena, falters when he discovers her role in his sudden good fortune, and her intention to exploit the newly-acquired abilities he'd feared were the start of a mental breakdown.

But, it turns out both George and Serena are being twitched by a greater puppet master and ultimately, they must decide whose side they're on—those who want to combat Climate-Armageddon or the powerful leaders of the human race.

Order from Amazon: <u>mybook.to/TheFutureBrokers</u>
Paperback: ISBN 979-8723077676
eBook: ASIN B08Z9QYH5F

Printed in Great Britain
by Amazon

Printed in Great Britain
by Amazon

22596410R00076